A Bell for Christmas

The Miracle Series

Landria Onkka

outskirtspress
DENVER, COLORADO

This is a work of fiction. The events and characters described herein are imaginary and are not intended to refer to specific places or living persons. The opinions expressed in this manuscript are solely the opinions of the author and do not represent the opinions or thoughts of the publisher. The author has represented and warranted full ownership and/or legal right to publish all the materials in this book.

A Bell for Christmas
The Miracle Series
All Rights Reserved.
Copyright © 2016 Landria Onkka
v3.0

Cover Photo © 2016 thinkstockphotos.com. All rights reserved - used with permission.

This book may not be reproduced, transmitted, or stored in whole or in part by any means, including graphic, electronic, or mechanical without the express written consent of the publisher except in the case of brief quotations embodied in critical articles and reviews.

Outskirts Press, Inc.
http://www.outskirtspress.com

ISBN: 978-1-4787-7636-9

Outskirts Press and the "OP" logo are trademarks belonging to Outskirts Press, Inc.

PRINTED IN THE UNITED STATES OF AMERICA

There's a legend in Rosedale that homeless, Old Lady Bell comes from wealth. But then no one pays much attention to her and her pudgy Terrier who roam the streets of the small, southern town. That is, until Animal Control threatens to take the dog from Bell, and soft hearted attorneys Sarah Wright and John Rivera step in to help. Does Bell really live in the decayed mansion on the outskirts of town and what drove the former socialite into obscurity? They turn to family friend Judge Joe Conner for answers only to find out that he is reluctant to reveal details about Bell or his own mysterious past. What is the Judge withholding and why? What starts as an animal rescue turns into a mystery that Sarah and John are determined to unravel. A life threatening event leads them to a shocking discovery and an ending that surprises everyone. This Christmas romance will warm your heart and restore your faith in eternal love, hope, and miracles.

My Dedication

I dedicate this story to all of the wonderful people who rescue, care for, support, and restore the well being of animals worldwide. *Your dedication and love for Earth's beautiful creatures is amazing. My promise is that for every book sold, I will dedicate funds to an animal organization or cause and continue to support you as I always have.*

Contents

Chapter One	Life Is Good	1
Chapter Two	Food for Thought	14
Chapter Three	No Moon Walk Allowed	34
Chapter Four	Ghosts of the Past	43
Chapter Five	Hot Mulled Wine and a Secret or Two	55
Chapter Six	Nothing Like Popovers	69
Chapter Seven	Gus Makes a Great Shepherd's Pie	77
Chapter Eight	Queen Costello	91
Chapter Nine	Hidden Treasure	101
Chapter Ten	A Tall Order	111
Chapter Eleven	Emma to the Rescue	121
Chapter Twelve	An Even Bigger Surprise	135
Conclusion		147

Chapter One
Life Is Good

"Ping da la ping ping ping . . . Ping da la ping ping ping . . . Ping da la ping ping ping . . ."

Sarah turns over in her bed and groans. "No. Not yet." She squints at the cell phone that is now lit on her nightstand, announcing morning.

"Ping da la ping ping ping . . . SMACK!" Sarah grabs the phone and pushes her thumb on the finger print ID pad quickly shutting down the serene, but annoying wake up alarm. She turns back over on her stomach, pushing her face into the pillow. Her long, blond hair is skewed like a string mop thrown haphazardly.

"Who picked that annoying alarm sound?" She pulls the covers up over her shoulders and settles back in.

"You did." John turns to face Sarah and pulls the tresses of hair off of her face. "Hey beautiful. We have a big case today. No time to lolly gag." He leans over and kisses Sarah's forehead.

"Lolly gag? What does that mean anyway? Lolly gag. Ugh! Can't we just call the courthouse and tell them we decided to sleep in a little bit later? We'll see them some time this afternoon." Sarah smiles, her eyes still closed.

"Oh, I'm sure Judge Conner will be happy to postpone the trial. Hon, why don't you give him a call and let me know how that goes." John grins, scoots to the edge of the bed and sits up. He leans over and touches his toes and gives out a big sigh. "Ohhh, that feels good." He then turns around and watches Sarah, whose breathing deepens. "O.K. Princess. I'll go start the coffee and I expect to hear that shower running shortly." He watches her as she continues to breath steadily with no response. John leans over and nudges her shoulder. "Hey, Sarah. Don't fall back asleep now! We need to be sharp today."

"BudIrilly wannashust schlipin." Sarah mumbles with her face totally buried in her pillow.

"What?" John stands and slides his feet into his slippers.

"I said I'm getting up." She answers slowly, as she turns on her back and rubs her eyes.

"O.K. I'll see you in a few minutes. I'll get the coffee brewing. Now get cracking counselor!" John smacks her butt.

Sarah mumbles again and turns on her side, watching him. "Coffee. Must have coffee."

"I'm on it my dear." John puts on his robe and shuffles down the stairs. The wooden floors of the old bungalow squeak with every step. He stops on one of the steps and gives it a couple of pushes with his foot. It squeaks each time. John smiles and continues down the stairs.

Sarah scoots to the edge of the bed and yawns, stretching her arms over her head. A large, black Labrador retriever curled up on the floor rolls on his back and wags his tail. "Baxter! You too?! Lucky pup! At least one of us gets to sleep in!"

"You'd better be in that shower!" John shouts from the kitchen. "The coffee's brewing!"

Sarah walks into the bathroom and turns on the bathtub faucet. The shower head immediately sprays on her face, causing her to jump back. She quickly shuts the shower curtain and looks in the mirror, grabs a towel and wipes water from her eyes. "O.K. girl, get it together." She grabs her tooth brush and scrubs her teeth before hopping into the now steamy, hot shower.

John stands in the kitchen, watching the coffee drip into the glass pot and sniffs the toasty aroma. He walks to the glass doors that overlook the backyard and sees the icy landscape. "Oh boy, we'll need to bundle up today." John makes his way back up the stairs and into the bathroom, now steamed up, and uses his robe sleeve to wipe a circle on the fogged up mirror.

Sarah sticks her head out of the shower curtain. "Showered and ready to face the world!" She steps out and wraps herself in a large towel. "Brrr!"

"Brrr is right. Dress warm. The temperatures are dropping out there." John brushes his teeth while Sarah makes her way into her bedroom closet. She swings open the door and walks in, staring at the lineup of suits. "John! Black or black?"

"Definitely the black one!" he shouts as he steps into the shower.

Sarah thinks for a moment, pulls out a grey suit and places it on the bed. She heads back to the bathroom and pulls her hair up into a twist, securing it with bobby pins.

"The coffee should be ready, Sarah!" John shouts over the pounding water.

"I'm right here, dear." Sarah says as she finishes pinning her hair in place.

John sticks his head out from the shower curtain. "Oh, sorry." He lowers his voice. "The coffee should be finished brewing. Why don't you go get yourself a cup and I'll meet you downstairs. I'm thinking that we can grab something to eat at the courthouse."

"Sounds good to me." Sarah walks back to the bedroom where she dresses into a black turtleneck sweater and her grey suit. She walks to a full length mirror and takes a look. "Showtime!" She heads downstairs where she prepares two coffee cups. Baxter makes an appearance, wagging his tail in anticipation of breakfast. Sarah pours his dog chow into a large bowl and in less than a minute the food is devoured.

Sarah watches him and shakes her head. "My word, Baxter. You'd think we never feed you!" She lets Baxter out the kitchen door. He rushes down the porch steps and into the backyard where he takes off in pursuit of a squirrel that easily escapes.

"Bax doing his business?" John appears, fully dressed in a suit.

Tall, with wide shoulders and a fit physique, he looks more like a GQ model than a small southern town attorney. His dark brown hair is cut short and complements his bright blue eyes, high cheek bones and square jaw. He picks up a cup and fills it with coffee.

"Yep. You ready?" Sarah leans against the counter and watches him.

"Hey, I thought you were wearing a black suit," John looks at Sarah's dark grey tweed jacket and skirt. He looks down at his own dark grey suit.

"I was. I decided to be a little different today. Pretty exciting, huh?" She laughs. "We'll be coordinated. I think it's cute."

"Attorneys aren't supposed to be cute," John grins as he reaches into the refrigerator for cream.

"It'll catch them off guard," she smirks, still watching John as he prepares his coffee.

"If only that's all it took to win a case!" John looks at Sarah. One corner of his mouth is up, revealing a dimple.

Sarah continues to watch him as he stirs his coffee and raises his cup to drink. "Have I told you how much I love you?"

John gives her a look of surprise. "Why Sarah Wright! Actually, you haven't. Not today, that is. Have I told you how beautiful you are?"

"Why John Rivera, a girl can't hear that enough. Oh, and its Sarah *Rivera*." She smiles, sips her coffee and walks to the glass door, watching Baxter sniff around the backyard. "You know what we're fast approaching?"

"Christmas?" John raises his eyebrows. "Wait, wait. I know. It's the two-year anniversary of our first case together! Saving Mr. Landis from going to jail for putting a Christmas tree on his roof!"

Sarah gives him a grin and places one hand on her hip.

"You remember?" he continues. "The rooftop Christmas tree? That's a case you won't see on any other attorney's resume! Who could forget. Good ol' Judge Joe made us work right up until Christmas!" He pauses and grins.

Sarah smiles. "Yes, I remember the situation quite well, thank you."

"No? That's not it? Hmmmm. Let me think. Oh, right! I get to play Santa again at the town tree lighting!" Sarah sighs and shakes her head. John watches her and raises an eyebrow. "*Or*, our one-year wedding anniversary, perhaps?"

"Of course, smarty. My sense of humor isn't exactly at its peak this early in the morning. How shall we celebrate? I mean, besides the fact that it falls on Christmas Eve." Sarah looks back at Baxter, still sniffing around and unaffected by the frigid temperatures.

"I don't know. We *are* expected at your parents that night, hon. I thought we could do something special before hand." John sips on his coffee and shrugs his shoulders.

"Yeah, I was thinking about that. Maybe it wasn't so smart to get married on Christmas Eve! It's like having a birthday on Christmas. It could get lost."

"I don't think so! Come here!" John puts his coffee down and stretches his arms out. Sarah walks to him and he wraps her up in a tight hug. "Of course it was smart! It's a perfect day for our anniversary. Besides, neither of us will ever forget it! We'll come up with something special. With an anniversary on Christmas Eve, we'll need to get creative!" John takes Sarah by the shoulders and pulls her away, looking straight into her eyes. "I have the feeling that it's going to be a very special night. Don't you worry Mrs. Rivera."

Sarah kisses him. "I won't. As long as we're together, I'll be a happy girl." They hug and hear a bark. "Oh! Baxter! I'll let him in. You get our coats and let's go show 'em how small town attorneys play with big corporations."

"Deal." John places his coffee cup in the dishwasher and heads to the coat closet near the living room door. He looks outside at the cars parked along the street, covered with frost that sparkle like tiny diamonds as the morning sun reflects off of them. A light snow covers the ground. John pulls out their coats along with gloves and scarves. "We're going to need these," he mumbles to himself.

Sarah joins him and they bundle up. "Bye Baxter!" John leans over and rubs the happy dog's head. Baxter's entire body wobbles back and forth, controlled by his wildly wagging tail.

"Darling? Ladies first." John opens the front door and the two make their way to their ice covered car parked in the driveway.

John and Sarah make the short drive to the courthouse, stopping at the final intersection before they turn into the parking lot.

"We probably should have walked," John says. "It's not even far enough for the car to heat up!" He begins to accelerate and suddenly slams on the brakes. "What the?"

Without warning, an older lady and her pudgy dog step in front of the car, on their way across the intersection.

"That's Bell and Emma!" Sarah exclaims. "Geez! She's going to get hit one of these days. She didn't even look!"

"No kidding. What is she doing out in these frigid temperatures anyway? She needs to be inside somewhere," John says, waiting for the elderly woman to make it safely to the other side of the street.

"Gosh John, Bell's getting up there in age. Do you know that I remember her roaming the streets for at least ten years?" Sarah shares.

"Has it been that long?" John shakes his head.

"It has. Makes me sad," Sarah watches the woman shuffle down the sidewalk on her way without so much as a glance back. The couple sit at the stop sign watching her. "Come on, hon. We need to get to the courthouse if we're going to grab something to eat before the case," Sarah says.

"Yeah. Sure." John proceeds, still watching the woman make her way down the snowy sidewalk, the little dog waddling next to her.

The couple quickly proceed to the parking lot where they gather their belongings and head into the building. On the front lawn, the courthouse Christmas tree stands tall and proud. Enormous red, silver, and green bulbs adorn the strong boughs that stretch wide. John and Sarah make their way up the steps and into the historic, brick building. They check in at the front counter where behind it sits a cheery, rosy cheeked middle aged woman.

"Claire! Good morning!" Sarah says as she grabs a pen and signs in.

"Good morning you two! It's a chilly one at that!" she responds.

"It certainly is." John rubs his gloved hands together.

"Big case today?" Claire asks, handing them a folder of papers.

"Pretty big," Sarah answers. "The Donner case." Sarah takes the folder.

"Ah, yes. Taking on the big medical device company. You're in courtroom 6B." Claire nods her head. "Good luck!"

"Thanks Claire." John takes the folder from Sarah.

"Oh, and Sarah!" Claire shouts as the two make their way down the hall. Sarah turns to look back at her. "It's so nice to see you on time these days." Claire smiles as Sarah gives her a grin.

John looks at Sarah with a questioning expression. "What was that about?"

"Oh, before we got married, I was often . . . never mind." Sarah hustles down the hall, avoiding the question and smiling to herself.

The two make their way to the cafeteria for a quick breakfast. The room is full of attorneys, defendants, and plaintiffs eating, drinking coffee, and chatting about their cases while they wait on their allotted trial times. Sarah and John step into a small line that leads past a display case loaded with muffins, bagels, fruits and other fast breakfast items.

"I can cook up a breakfast biscuit if you'd like," the young man behind the counter offers. "Biscuit, scrambled eggs and bacon, plus grits on the side. Y'all want me to make you one?"

"I think we'll stick with the muffins. We're in a bit of a rush. But thanks for the offer," John says as he eyes the display. "We'll take two blueberry muffins, please." John looks to Sarah for confirmation. She nods her head in agreement.

The young man plucks them off of the shelf and places them in a paper bag, handing it to John. The two shuffle forward and fill paper coffee cups from large, metal dispensers. John pours cream in his while Sarah fixes her own when she suddenly feels a tap on her shoulder.

"Hey Sarah." A man stands behind her in an expensive navy suit, a crisp white shirt, and light blue striped tie. He is an attractive man with salt and pepper hair, looking very professional.

"Derek! Hi. We were just having a quick breakfast before the case. I'd ask you to join, but John and I are going to go over a few details beforehand. How are you?" Sarah asks.

"Doing great. Listen, it's about the case. I'd like to have a word with you both. May we take a seat over in the corner?" he asks.

"Why sure. We'll finish up here and join you," Sarah says, giving John an inquisitive look.

Derek makes his way to the corner of the cafeteria and claims a table. John moves to the cashier and turns to Sarah as he pulls out his wallet. "Are you thinking what I'm thinking?"

"I am, and I hope we're right. There's usually one reason a defendant's attorney wants to meet prior to walking into the courtroom. If Derek wants to strike up a deal, I hope it's a fair one. They really don't have much of a case, but they have a lot of fire power behind them. Maybe they're going to do the right thing," Sarah says, looking for John's reaction.

"Don't count on that. They have deep pockets and this case is more about protecting their reputation. You know it's bad press when one of their devices is defective. Mr. Donner will be lucky to walk again. Come on. Let's get over there and see what he has to say." John finishes paying for their breakfast and they join Derek.

"You probably have an idea of what I'm about to propose," Derek begins.

"Possibly. Go ahead," John prompts him.

"My client has agreed to settle out of court. We won't make this a bidding game. They're willing to award the settlement that Mr. Donner requested including attorney's fees." Derek blankly stares at the two.

"That's it?" John asks.

"Yep. That's it," Derek responds, folding his hands on the table.

"No negotiations? What made them change their mind?" Sarah asks.

"When I told my client that they were dealing with a former partner of one of the most prestigious law firms in the southeast, they took notice. I explained that John had quite a reputation as a winning corporate attorney and they decided that maybe Rosedale wasn't going to be such an easy touch." Derek looked apologetic.

"Hey, Derek, we get it. It wouldn't be the first time a small town attorney's experience has been underestimated. I'm just pleased that Mr. Donner's case is now off the table. Did you bring documents for us to review?" John asks.

"Yes, I've prepared everything and have it with me. If you're in agreement, we can go over this with Judge Conner." Derek pulls documents from his briefcase and slides them across the table toward John and Sarah.

"Judge Conner will be pleased that his workload just got lighter." Sarah takes the papers and opens the folder. She begins to read over them.

"So, John, how's it going now that you two have your own practice together? Do you miss corporate law?" Derek asks.

"It's great," John answers, looking at Sarah. "I get to work with my beautiful wife, we pick and choose our cases, and frankly it's a lot less stressful. Nope, I don't miss corporate law at all," John admits.

"Yes, he came to the light!" Sarah squeezes his arm.

"Yeah, it's a lot nicer on this side of the fence. Derek, thanks for making this happen. Sarah and I'll finish our muffins here and we'll meet you in the courtroom before our scheduled time." John stands and extends his hand.

"My pleasure. But, you don't need to thank me. You know I would have gone toe to toe with you. Off the record, I think that they made a sound decision and I wish Mr. Donner all the best." Derek stands and shakes John's hand. "Sarah? It's a pleasure." Sarah shakes his hand, also. "I'll see you two shortly." Derek makes his way out of the cafeteria, while the couple remain at the table with their breakfast.

"That was a nice surprise," John says, unwrapping his muffin.

"That was pretty impressive!" Sarah adds.

"Impressive?" John asks.

"Yes. He said it. Your representation of Mr. Donner had a big influence on their decision." Sarah takes a bite of muffin.

"You mean 'our' representation. There are two of us here," John reminds her.

"Yes, but you're the former corporate attorney with the winning track record, on some pretty big cases I might add. I'm proud to have you as my partner!" Sarah raises her eyebrows as she continues to eat, giving John a sheepish grin.

"Uh huh. Well, I'm happy to be your partner, darling. I can't take all of the credit for this case. Now finish that muffin and let's speak with Judge Joe."

"John, take the compliment and let's get out of here. I can finish this muffin later." Sarah grabs his hand and pulls him up.

"O.K., O.K. You're in charge. Do you have the documents?" John asks.

"Yep. We're all set. Come on handsome!" Sarah grabs John's arm.

They head back into the hallway and to courtroom 6B where they wait for Judge Joe to call up their case. Derek spots them and waives them to the front of the room and the Judge gestures for them to step forward.

"John and Sarah, Derek informed me that his client has agreed to a settlement. Please join me in my chambers." Judge Joe Conner, a portly, balding, middle aged man stands at about 5'9" and is almost as wide. His full face and rosy cheeks are disarming. A friend of the family, Sarah has known Judge Joe since she was a child and interned with him while in law school. He has always been a source of wisdom and guidance for her, and a pillar of the community. However, despite Judge Conner's kind demeanor, he doesn't play favorites and is known for being a tough but fair man.

The four convene in the Judge's chambers. "Please everyone, take a seat and let's get down to business." Dressed in his robes, the Judge takes his seat at the opposite side of an overly large, mahogany desk. He settles into his chair and gives a big sigh. "O.K. what do we have here?" He pulls out his reading glasses and examines papers that Derek and Sarah place before him.

"Are there any issues with the settlement?" He continues to examine the papers.

"We're in agreement on all points," John says, leaning forward. "Is that correct, Derek?"

"Yes. Judge Conner, my client has agreed to grant the settlement as stated. We'll need to work out the details of the payments," Derek responds.

"John and Sarah, that's quite an offer. Counselor Stanford, I'm pleased at this decision." The Judge leans forward and smiles at Derek.

"Your Honor, you see, I informed them that we were dealing with John Rivera," Derek says.

"Ah ha, I see," the Judge laughs. "Big business thought that small town lawyers wouldn't be a challenge. Congratulations, John and Sarah. Counselor Stanford, we'll schedule a future review until which time this case is finalized and Mr. Donner is receiving restitution." The Judge pauses and looks at Sarah. "How is Mr. Donner, Sarah?"

"He's still hospitalized, but recovering. He continues to struggle with his ability to walk, but will be going into therapy shortly," she shares.

"Then he and his family will need all of that settlement money, so let's wrap up the details soon, shall we?" The Judge looks at Derek.

"Yes, your Honor," Derek answers.

"Good. I'll need signatures from all of you and look forward to seeing you back soon." Everyone stands and shakes hands with the Judge and one another. "Derek, thank you. Sarah and John, could you please stay for a moment?" the Judge requests.

Sarah and John thank Derek and settle back into their chairs. Judge Joe waits until Derek has collected his belongings and leaves the chambers. He leans back in his chair and rubs his belly. "So, the newlyweds! Christmas is almost here. How do you plan on celebrating your first year together? It seems that you have a lot of 'firsts' coming up. Your new law practice, your anniversary. Sarah, I haven't seen you in here with many forlorn pro bono clients lately. What gives?"

"John and I were just trying to decide what to do for our anniversary. I'm sure we'll come up with something exciting. As for my pro bono cases, I guess Rosedale isn't in need of being rescued lately," Sarah shrugs her shoulders.

"Except for the animals. Sarah and I still donate our time to the Rosedale Animal Rescue," John adds.

"How is that rescue that you adopted? What's his name? Bassett, or," the Judge thinks.

John laughs. "Baxter! Yes, Baxter's still happy and healthy. Thanks for asking. He'll be Santa's Helper at the annual town Christmas tree lighting, as you know."

"Oh, that's right. Ol' Baxter will be sitting at your side. So nice that you'll be playing Santa again this year," the Judge says.

Sarah leans forward. "Judge Joe, will you be joining our family for Christmas?"

"I certainly plan on it. I look forward to visiting with your parents as always. I'll give your Dad a call to let him know." The Judge smiles and leans back looking relaxed. "Well, I just wanted to visit for a moment. I'm proud of you both and I enjoy seeing you in my courtroom on the same side for a change!" He laughs. "Now, I have to get back in there and straighten out this town." He stands up and walks around the table, hugs Sarah and shakes John's hand.

The Judge walks back into the courtroom while Sarah and John head to the hallway.

"I guess we have some extra time on our hands. I'm going back to the office," John shares.

"I know it's crazy to say this since it's so cold out, but I'm going to get a run in. I have cabin fever. I'll take care of Baxter when I get home and meet you at the office in a couple of hours." Sarah takes the documents from John's hands. "You O.K. walking to the office?"

"I can handle a couple of blocks. You've got the car keys. I'll see you later. We have a 1:00 p.m. back here, so don't be late." John kisses Sarah's cheek.

"Deal." Sarah heads for the car and back to their home.

Chapter Two
Food for Thought

Sarah picks up her pace, taking in a deep breath of the crisp winter air. Her long, blond hair is pulled back in a pony tail. She grabs her knitted cap and pulls it further down over her ears and forehead and rubs her thick mittens together, attempting to generate heat. She runs through the neighborhood, up and down the streets, viewing the southern homes both quaint and grand, now decorated with Christmas wreaths, roping and an occasional obnoxious, oversized lawn decoration.

As Sarah continues running, she sees a man walk to his mailbox, placing a letter inside. On top of his small home is a lit Christmas tree. "Hello Mr. Landis!" she shouts, waving.

"Hello Sarah," he waves back. "I hope you're bundled up properly! It's unusually cold for our southern town!"

"It is! And I am! Mr. Landis, the tree looks great!" she points to the roof.

"Thanks, Sarah! Keeping up the tradition!" He beams with pride. "Oh Sarah, can you stop for a moment? I have something I've been meaning to give you."

Sarah stops and approaches him. "What's that Mr. Landis?"

He walks into the house and in a few moments reappears with an object in his hands. "Sarah, I want to give this back to you." Mr. Landis opens his hand to reveal a dazzling, crystal star that appears to glow independently.

"That's the star that I placed on your rooftop Christmas tree! The one that Judge Joe gave me as a Christmas gift," Sarah says, mesmerized by its beauty.

"It is." Mr. Landis nods and gives her a big smile.

Sarah's thoughts go back to the beautiful star that Judge Joe had given her two Christmas's ago. A gift, that she somehow knew carried magical powers, she placed it on the top of Mr. Landis's rooftop tree in hopes that it would bless his home. And it surely did. Mr. Landis and many others received a miracle that year which surprised everyone. Everyone but Judge Joe, that is. But then the Judge has his mysterious ways that can never quite be explained. All Sarah knows is that good things happen around Judge Joe and whomever possesses the Christmas star.

"Mr. Landis, I can't accept this! It was meant for you!" She extends her hand, attempting to give it back.

"Oh, Sarah, I don't need the star. It's done its job here! You keep it. You'll find a good use for it!" He pushes her hand back.

Sarah holds the star with both hands on her heart and smiles at him.

"Sometimes I would come outside at night and just look at it dazzling on top of the tree. It always gave me peace. I think it has magical powers." He pauses and smiles. "Perhaps it's just a symbol of hope. That's all we need, isn't it?"

"Yes, Mr. Landis. Sometimes that *is* all that we need."

"It's time to send it on to someone else," he smiles.

"Thank you." Sarah carefully places the star in her pocket. "I'll be sure to do that."

"Oh, and Sarah, will you and your husband be at the Christmas block party? I'm holding it at my house this year!" he states proudly.

"Mr. Landis, we wouldn't miss it! We'll see you there," she responds.

"Wonderful. Now you go on your way young lady! I know you have a busy schedule!" Mr. Landis walks back to his porch and turns around. "Oh and Sarah," he pauses and smiles. "Thank you for caring about an old man and his dreams." He waves.

Sarah smiles and waves back. "It was good to see you, Mr. Landis!" She begins her jog, keeping a steady pace until finally, she arrives at her destination. She stops at a simple, cinder block building painted a bright yellow with a wall size cartoon painting of a happy dog dancing. Underneath, in big red letters are the words 'Rosedale Animal Rescue.' Sarah smiles, steps inside and up to the reception counter.

"I like the new artwork, Ellen!" Sarah comments.

"Isn't it adorable? We love it. Local artists teamed up to paint it and Rosedale high school students pitched in. I think it's a happy message, don't you?" Ellen, the receptionist and a rescue volunteer responds.

"It certainly is! Now we just have to get happy dogs into more happy homes!"

"And don't forget the horses, cats, hamsters, and," Ellen adds.

"Hamsters?" Sarah laughs.

"Yes! We took in a couple of homeless hamsters!" Ellen smiles. "Actually, they're warm and snug at my house."

"You're sweet, Ellen." Sarah rubs her mittens together. "Woo! That temperature's dropping!" She hops up and down to keep warm. "It's not too cold for the pups though. I think they'll love it. Make sure you give me some big guys with lots of fur!"

"How many today, Sarah?" Ellen asks. "Can you handle three? Molly, Mickey, and Mo are due for a nice outing!"

"I can handle it. Bring 'em out!" Sarah says, bouncing up and down on her tennis shoes and rubbing her hands.

"How's the law practice going?" Ellen asks. "Are you and John keeping busy?"

"Yes! Business is good! In fact, I need to get into the office after our run, so I'll see you in about an hour."

"That's fine. Whatever time you can give them Sarah, is much appreciated. I'll bring 'em out while you warm up." Ellen walks to the kennel door and disappears.

In the corner is a small Christmas tree, strung with multi-colored, flashing lights. It is the same artificial tree that Rosedale Rescue has put up for as long as Sarah can remember. Each year it gathers more ornaments donated from well wishers, so numerous that they obscure the branches. Sarah smiles, examining some of them, consisting of animals, commemorative ornaments, misfit and humorous pieces.

A cold breeze blows through the room and Sarah looks toward the front door to see old lady Bell enter. She is shabbily dressed in a long wool, frayed overcoat, knit hat with ear flaps, gloves with cut out fingers, and old worn work boots. As always, she shuffles to the counter where the large, glass jar of dog treats sits. She reaches deep inside and pulls out a handful of bones which she stashes in her pockets. Today, she takes a second helping. Bell gives Sarah a quick glance, keeping her head down.

"Good morning, Bell," Sarah kindly says. Bell ignores her and slowly shuffles back outside where her portly Terrier Emma sits waiting and wagging her stubby tail.

Ellen appears with the three, happy and jumping dogs. "Here you go, Sarah! You take whatever time you need, and hopefully you can wear them out!"

Sarah laughs as the three dogs greet her with licks and wags. "O.K., kids! I can see that we need to run off some energy this morning!" She crouches down and pets each animal, attempting to settle them down. "Hey Ellen, Bell just came in here."

"Oh, yes. Making her daily visit for Emma's treats. She's early today." Ellen takes her place back behind the counter.

"John and I almost ran her and Emma over this morning. She stepped right in front of our car and didn't even look back. I worry about her with this cold weather and all. She's looking so thin. Does anyone know where she goes at night?" Sarah continues to pet the dogs.

"Funny you should mention it, but I was told that there was a complaint from someone who's concerned about the dog. Apparently they think that Bell isn't taking care of her properly, being a street person and all." Ellen shakes her head with a look of concern.

"Oh really? All of these years and I don't think *anyone* has ever figured out where Bell goes at night. Between Emma and Bell, I think *Emma* is the one receiving the best treatment. It'd be a shame to see Bell lose the only thing that means anything to her in this world. I was just telling John that I remember seeing Bell wander the streets for years!"

"My guess is that you know the town legend?" Ellen leans across the reception counter and lowers her voice despite the fact that no one else is in the room.

"I do." Sarah pulls treats from the jar and feeds it to the three pups. "She supposedly comes from a wealthy family and wanders the streets for no good reason. I assume that she's suffering from some kind of emotional or mental illness."

"Yep. That's what they say," Ellen confirms. "We've heard that story for years. Yet no one knows where Bell lives or where she comes from. Every day she's here for Emma's treats and wanders the town. I heard that John's the only one she acknowledges." Ellen leans further out, sticking her head in to the reception area, waiting for Sarah's response.

"It's true. John occasionally meets her at *The Pot Hole* and treats her and Emma to a pot pie. Mostly Emma, actually. That started a couple of years ago, when John moved back to Rosedale, before we got married," Sarah reminds her.

"Whatever do they talk about?" Ellen asks.

"Apparently, not much. John does the talking and she sits there smiling and feeding Emma most of her pot pie. She really took to him. He doesn't ask her questions on purpose. He just wants to get some decent food in her and the fewer questions, the better. You know how she is. No one can even get eye contact with her and when she speaks, it's mumbling," Sarah reminds Ellen.

"I can't say that I blame Bell. We *all* took to John!" Ellen giggles like a school girl. "I'm just worried that the authorities are going to pick up little Emma and that will be the end of old lady Bell." Ellen shakes her head again.

"Ellen, how did you hear about the complaint?" Sarah asks.

"One of our volunteers went to the Rosedale Animal Control to pick up a couple of dogs and a worker there mentioned it," Ellen responds.

"So, what's going to be done? Is it a serious complaint?" Sarah asks becoming more concerned.

"Oh, it's serious. They're going to look into it. It's not a case of abuse, so much as they claim neglect, assuming that she's homeless. Sarah, that would break Bell's heart to lose Emma." Ellen tears up.

"Let me see what I can find out. It would help to know the facts. John and I can do a bit of research. For now, I have anxious puppies that need a good run!" Sarah walks toward the door as the dogs jump in anticipation. She opens it and they bolt for the sidewalk. "See you in an hour!" Sarah yells as she runs out, being pulled by the energetic crew.

As Sarah leaves the building she looks around to see if Bell is in the area, but she is no where in sight. Sarah slowly jogs until she and the pups settle into a steady pace. The locals wave to her, along with store owners and business people walking to their destinations. As the dogs eventually slow down, she finishes their hour with a brisk walk and returns them to the Rescue, tired and happy. Sarah jogs back to her home where she showers and changes into her suit.

Ready for work, Sarah drives to a small, one story office building and parks in the lot behind it. She quickly makes her way inside and down a hall where on the entrance is a sign, "Rivera and Rivera Attorneys at Law." She touches the sign and smiles before entering the reception area where a petite Asian woman sits at a desk.

"Good morning, Samantha! Is there any coffee left?" Sarah takes off her coat and hangs it on a coat rack in the entrance.

"It's not morning, Sarah. It's noon. You have an hour before your next case," Samantha corrects her, in a strong Asian accent. She looks at Sarah, shaking her head. "You two drink a *whole* lot of coffee. A whole lot! I brewed a fresh pot for Mr. Rivera. He drink *way* too much coffee too! You must never sleep!"

"Yes, well there's no doubt about that. Is Mr. Rivera in?" Sarah asks as she sorts through mail stacked on Samantha's desk.

"Mr. Rivera is busy in his office. Just like you. Always busy, busy! But I don't complain. Busy is good. Sarah and John busy, Samantha busy!"

"Hopefully we'll continue to be busy. Samantha, may I have my schedule for the week?" Sarah asks as she opens an envelope.

"Already sitting on your desk." Samantha smiles with pride.

"Of course it is." Sarah looks up from her mail and smiles back. "Thank you." Sarah walks to her husband's office and peeks in. "Good afternoon, darling!"

John sits at his desk reading and looks up, giving Sarah a big smile. "You made it back! How was your run? Did you wear the dogs out?"

"That's a big task. More like the dogs wore me out! I saw Mr. Landis this morning. He has his tree up," she smiles.

"Good ol' Mr. Landis. Glad to know that he's keeping up the tradition. Samantha made a fresh pot of coffee."

"So I heard. 'You drink too much coffee! You never sleep!'" Sarah mimics Samantha.

"She's right. We never sleep!" John stands and walks to the other side of the desk. "It wouldn't hurt if we cut back. Maybe we should switch to tea." He takes Sarah's face in his hands and gives her a big kiss.

"Why counselor, do you think that's appropriate at the workplace?" Sarah asks pretending to be serious.

"I most certainly do." John grabs her hand and walks her into the hallway. "Don't speak until you've had your caffeine. By the way, tea isn't such a bad idea." They walk into a small kitchen where John pulls a cup out of the cupboard, fills it and hands it to Sarah.

"Thanks, hon." She pauses. "John, when was the last time you saw Bell?"

"Bell? Sweet, mysterious, old lady Bell? You mean besides almost running her over this morning? Gosh, we met up at *The Pot Hole* a week ago. Why?" He leans against the wall and crosses his arms.

"Well, Ellen at the Rescue told me that someone had made a report to the authorities that Emma should be removed." Sarah takes the coffee and blows on it, releasing steam.

"What? That dog gets far better care than Bell. You know how much she loves that dog. It would devastate her." John stands straight, uncrossing his arms.

"I know, but anyone who doesn't know Bell wouldn't know that. In fact, even those of us who know her have no idea where she lives." Sarah pauses and stares at John. "I have to admit that I've had my own concerns. That temperature has dropped and who knows where those two go at night."

"You know the stories. She's a wealthy heiress and wanders the streets for some unknown reason." John turns up a corner of his mouth. "Truthfully, Sarah, I don't believe a word of it. It doesn't make sense and I think we'd know if there was an estate that was missing its matriarch. I think it's just urban legend."

"Yeah. Ellen and I had this discussion. You know her better than anyone. You've gotten closer to her. No one's been able to do that. What does she say?" Sarah sips her coffee.

John thinks. "Well, I tell her stories and she giggles like a little girl. She's very sweet. I do all of the talking. I just try to keep her there long enough to feed her and Emma. As soon as that pot pie is finished she's off, sometimes even in the middle of one of my intriguing stories!"

"Amazing," Sarah smiles. "She doesn't know what she's missing. Seriously, John isn't there anything that she says?"

"Nothing. She just mumbles once in a while and I never ask her questions for fear that she'll leave without eating."

"That's probably why she trusts you. You may be the only non-threating person she comes in contact with, who doesn't judge her." Sarah thinks for a moment. "John, isn't there some tidbit that could give a clue as to where she's from, or where she goes?"

"Nothing. I'm sorry, Sarah. I wish I had answers." He watches her face and sees that she is concerned. "Hey." John puts his arm around her and walks her into the hall. "If you're that worried about Bell and Emma, we'll look into it. I have the feeling that there's a wise Judge that can give us some insight. We'll figure something out." They walk to Sarah's office where John stops. "Gather your things and get ready. We need to head over to the courthouse. I have everything prepared but I need you to be focused."

Sarah nods her head. "Yeah, I'm O.K. I just worry about her, you know?"

"I think you're more worried about that dog!" John smiles. "I mean it, Sarah. We'll check out the situation. Get your game face on for now, O.K.?"

"I will. Give me a few minutes and we can head out." Sarah takes a seat at her desk and pulls a file from her brief case. She reviews the documents and finishes her coffee, staring out the window in deep thought.

"Andy! What are you doing up there? The tree's perfect!" Sarah shouts to a man towering on a ladder at the top of the courthouse Christmas tree.

"We have a string of lights out Miss Sarah! Can't have a string of lights out! You know Miss Claire and the Judge won't have that! Miss Claire sent me out here to get it fixed before dusk," Andy shouts. "She said she don't want to see my mug 'til I got all the lights shinin'!"

"She looks pretty, Andy! Keep up the good work," John yells.

"Thank you, Mr. John! She gets bigger every year! I'm gonna' need a crane soon!" Andy pokes at the string of lights and twists each to see which one is burned out. "Mr. John! I hear you're back this year as Santa at the town tree lighting!"

"Shhhhh! I have no idea what you're talking about!" John teases.

"Well, Marla and I are bringin' the kids out to visit you, or Santa. Get ready, we have six now!" he laughs.

"I look forward to it!" John shouts back.

"Send Marla our good wishes!" Sarah yells.

Andy waves and nods. "I sure will!"

Sarah and John make their way into the courthouse and sign in.

"Nora Emmons is already just outside the courtroom waiting for you," Claire reveals, giving them a frown.

"What's that look?" Sarah asks.

"Oh, you'll find out. She's a nervous wreck. I wished her good luck and told her that I hoped she'd be out of jail in time for Christmas," Claire says with a big grin.

"You didn't get that poor woman all riled up," John says hiding a smile.

"Oh Claire! That was down right cruel!" Sarah shakes her head. "What are we going to do with you?"

"I don't know! Ask Judge Conner. He has a few ideas. Said he'd string me up on that Christmas tree on the front lawn if I didn't behave!" She smirks.

"Well, you keep this up and we might be helping him do just that!" Sarah teases.

Claire hands Sarah a stack of documents. "Courtroom 2B. Good luck!"

"Thanks, Claire." John says as they turn and head down the hall. "And *try* to behave!"

John and Sarah find Nora Emmons waiting for them outside of the appropriate room. She sees the couple and runs to them.

"I'm so glad you're here!" Nora puts her hand to her forehead.

"Nora, are you ready?" Sarah asks.

"I am," Nora says and then grabs Sarah's arm. "Oh Sarah, I'm so nervous and embarrassed! Isn't there another way to do this?"

"Nora, I'm afraid not. You can't just go on someone's property and start cutting down their trees! If you stand in front of the Judge, you'll have a chance to speak for yourself and tell him that this was just a mistake. He may show some compassion. Being here in person demonstrates that you're remorseful. That, and a big apology to William. I'm sure that this will be easily resolved." Sarah takes Nora's hand. "Come on, Nora. John and I will be with you the entire time so you have nothing to fear. Just make sure that you speak with sincerity whenever you're given the opportunity. You don't have to be formal about anything. That's Judge Joe in there and he'd rather hear the truth."

"I just can't go to jail for Christmas!" Nora cries.

"Nora, Claire was having fun with you. No one's going to jail." Sarah and John look at one another and shake their heads.

"Oh, that woman!" Nora exclaims.

"Just relax. You can do this, Nora," John assures her.

"Oh, I feel so silly! What was I thinking?" Nora clasps their hands tightly. She is noticeably upset but follows the couple into the courtroom, never letting go of their hands. They walk her to the front of the room, take a seat on a bench and are soon called before Judge Joe.

"Good afternoon, Judge," Sarah smiles as she stands and walks to the front of the room.

"Well, young lady, are you ready to begin?" The Judge sits in the front of the courtroom looking like a masterful King, taking up every inch of his chair. He places his reading glasses on and peers down at a piece of paper that sits before him. "Let's begin proceedings. William Sunderland vs Nora Emmons." Judge Joe looks up as John, Sarah, and Nora walk to the Judge podium.

"Mrs. Emmons, I see that you trespassed on Mr. Sunderland's

property, trimmed several of the bushes in his backyard, and took a chainsaw to several small trees." Attendants in the courtroom giggle. The Judge looks up and stares at her. "Mrs. Emmons, now why on earth would you cut down Mr. Sunderland's trees and trim his bushes?"

Mrs. Emmons who was staring at the floor, raises her head and sighs. "Your honor, Mr. Sunderland has never taken care of his landscaping. His trees and bushes are a mess and were an eyesore. I simply took it upon myself to do a little trimming. Here! I took pictures and you can see for yourself how nice it looks!" She extends her hand, holding a stack of photos. The Judge takes them and reviews each.

"Your honor," John interrupts. "Mrs. Emmons had the best of intentions. She was simply being a friendly neighbor and unfortunately overextended her neighborly generosity. Mr. Sunderland, I'm afraid did not agree with her actions. It *was* wrong and we are not here to tell you anything different. She is more than willing to make amends for her actions."

"Mr. Sunderland, are those bushes really that important to you? Granted, Mrs. Emmons had no business trespassing, much less altering your landscaping. However, it appears to me that considering the condition of your property, a slight improvement may have been made. Couldn't we just agree to have Mrs. Emmons replace whatever it was that she damaged or altered?"

"Your Honor." Mr. Sunderland sitting in the front of the courtroom stands. "Nora Emmons is just a nosey neighbor and she don't like how my property looks. So she decided to just go in my backyard with her clippers and do whatever she pleases!"

"Oh, Mr. Sunderland, I don't disagree with you. Despite the condition of your property, it doesn't give Mrs. Emmons the right to trespass and take yard duties into her own hands. However, may we come to a mutually agreed upon resolution? After all, Christmas is coming and wouldn't it be nice to show a little holiday spirit toward one another? Certainly we can work this out today to your satisfaction." The Judge sits back in his chair.

"Your Honor, I'm sure that our client, Mrs. Emmons would be happy to appease Mr. Sunderland and promises that she will not trespass on his property in the future." Sarah looks at Nora who nods her head in agreement.

"It's true, your honor. I promise not to trespass. I was only trying to help. You see, I'm an avid gardener and with the overgrown bushes and trees, I thought that I would trim them back and improve the view for the coming Spring. Judge Conner, I had to trim them back before the cold set in. Cold can damage them if you trim too late in the year, you know!"

"Well, Mrs. Emmons, I understand your logic in some bizarre way, but the fact remains that you simply can not make these decisions for other people and then act on them. I'm sure that you meant well but please, let's resolve this. May we? Mr. Sunderland, how may Mrs. Emmons make amends? Certainly you two can get along and can leave here as friends?" The Judge stares at the two.

"I suppose that I'd be might ready to mend ways if Nora cooked me a meal," he responds. The Judge, Nora, Sarah and John are silent, stunned at the odd request.

"Mr. Sunderland, did you say a meal?" Judge Joe has a look of amusement. Mr. Sunderland nods. "Any particular meal?" The Judge asks as John and Sarah give him a look of disbelief.

"Well, I don't have a gal in my life and it'd be really nice to have a home cooked meal. I don't mean comin' over to my place to cook or anything. I mean just droppin' off a meal. Maybe a casserole or somethin' nice like that. Somethin' made in a kitchen at home."

The courtroom is silent with the exception of a few more giggles as the Judge carefully contemplates this unusual request, and John fights to hide a smile. Sarah covers her face and snickers. Mrs. Emmons speaks. "Your Honor, I would be happy to cook Mr. Sunderland a meal. In fact, I would like to invite him to join my husband and I in our home for that meal, if he would like." She turns to Mr. Sunderland. "William, I'm so sorry for cutting back your bushes and trees. I only thought I was helping. They were *really* overgrown but, well, I had no right. If you're free this coming weekend, I'd be happy to cook you a casserole that you can take home, in addition to having you join us for dinner. Would that be acceptable?"

Mr. Sunderland is silent and strokes his chin in thought before responding. "What kinda' dinner?"

"Whatever you'd like," Nora answers with a grin.

"I'm pretty fond of lasagna. Can you make lasagna?" he asks with a serious expression.

"I make a very good lasagna, William. I'd be happy to make you lasagna," she says with a kind smile. "And you can take the leftovers home, too."

"Then it's settled. Mrs. Emmons will no longer trespass and will respect Mr. Sunderland's property and this weekend he will join Mrs. Emmons and her husband for lasagna," the Judge states.

"And don't forget that casserole!" William reminds him.

"Oh, yes, and the casserole. Mrs. Emmons will send Mr. Sunderland home with his casserole and any lasagna leftovers. Mrs. Emmons, are we clear on that?" Judge Joe asks.

"I'm happy to oblige, your Honor," Nora answers.

"Oh, and Mr. Sunderland, you may want to tend to your grounds. I appreciate that it is your property, but it would be neighborly of you to maintain your own bushes and trees. I don't want to see either of you in here again. Are we done?" The Judge looks at each of them.

"Yes, sir," Mr. Sunderland answers.

"Yes, your Honor," Nora replies.

"Thank you Judge," Mr. Sunderland smiles.

"Can you two please shake hands for me before you leave?" the Judge requests.

Nora extends both of her arms out toward Mr. Sunderland for a hug.

"Well, I don't think that I really want to hug . . . it's really not . . . Oh, O.K." Mr. Sunderland walks to her and she folds her arms around him. He reciprocates and they both begin to laugh. Tears well up in Nora's eyes.

"O.K., this is good. Now be kind to one another, respectful, and have a happy holiday season. Get out of my courtroom," the Judge smiles and shakes his head. "Never boring! Never boring!"

John and Sarah gather their paperwork and begin to leave. "A casserole. Who would have guessed. Leave it to Judge Joe," John says.

Sarah nods and grins. "Everyone just wants love."

"And a good home cooked meal, apparently." John leans in closer. "Hey, I'll finish the paperwork here. I have the Denin case on the 3rd floor. You can head back to the office and I'll see you at the house for dinner."

John walks Nora into the hallway. "Nora, you did great in there. I'm proud of you. Mr. Sunderland obviously just needed a little attention. Perhaps you can continue your amicable relationship with him."

"I will. Thank you, John." Nora shakes his hand then hugs him, wiping a tear from her eye.

"It was all you," John responds. "I'll finish up the paperwork. You can go home now. I just need to know that Mr. Sunderland got his lasagna dinner and his casserole." John pauses. "And keep your clippers in your potting shed!" He smiles.

"You can count on that!" Nora laughs. "I'll call you on Monday to let you know how it went." She turns and leaves the courthouse, waving to Claire on her way out.

"Did they keep you out of jail?" Claire teases.

"Oh you! I'll have a word with you later!" Nora laughs and exits.

"John!" John turns around to see Judge Joe standing behind him. "I was on my way to grab a sandwich. Care to join?"

A BELL FOR CHRISTMAS

"I have some time. Sure," John answers.

"May I join?" Sarah asks, as she exits the courtroom and walks up behind them.

"Of course, my dear. I didn't see you there," Judge Joe says as they make their way to the cafeteria.

"That certainly was something," the Judge gives a deep chuckle. "Just two neighbors not communicating. Now they're having dinner. Can you believe that?"

"Lasagna too! That's one for the books for sure," John shakes his head.

"Apparently, Nora has a reputation as a pretty good cook. John, you should have included us in that deal!" Sarah teases. They continue to walk down the hall until they reach the cafeteria and head toward the counter where an array of sandwiches are on display.

"Judge Joe," Sarah begins. "There's something I'd like to ask you. You know the Rosedale residents better than anyone, right?"

"Oh, I'd say that I have a pretty good handle on the characters in Rosedale. Yes, I do. Now, to say that I know *everyone* would be a stretch. Why do you ask?" Judge Joe has a look of curiosity as he steps up to the counter and orders his sandwich.

"Well, this morning I stopped by the Animal Rescue and Ellen told me that a concerned citizen reported that Bell may not be properly taking care of little Emma. You know, the elderly lady that roams the streets. Her and her little pudgy Terrier are getting some attention."

"Old lady Bell." The Judge strokes his chin and thinks. "Uh huh. I'm well aware of Bell and her Emma. That's a mystery to Rosedale. It certainly is, not that anyone takes notice. What's your concern, Sarah?"

"I can see why someone would think that Emma isn't receiving the best care. I mean it appears that Bell is homeless and it *is* unusually cold this winter. Well, I've heard that she comes from wealth and perhaps has some kind of emotional issues? I'm not sure, but I was wondering if perhaps you knew anything about her. I'm as concerned about animal welfare as anyone, but I would hate to see her lose the only precious thing in her life."

"Judge Joe, does anyone know her background or if she has a place to sleep at night? Is there anything that *you* know about her that might shed some light on the situation?" John watches as the Judge continues to stroke his chin and think.

"Well John, as you know, I was born and raised in Rosedale. Granted, I went away for a few years to Harvard for undergrad and then law school. Bell, well, she's always been somewhat of an enigma. I remember when Bell was a young woman. Why she was a mighty good looking gal at that!"

"Oh really? So, she's from Rosedale?" John's curiosity is now peaked.

"Oh, yes! It's true. Bell did come from a very wealthy family just on the outskirts of Rosedale. The Benton mansion was where Bell grew up." He nods his head.

"The big, dilapidated mansion by the old country church?" Sarah asks. John and Sarah look at each other in surprise. "On that huge overgrown piece of property?"

"Yep, that's the one. It was inhabited by the Benton family many years ago. The home dates back pre-civil war. It was once a grand place." The Judge pauses, pays for his sandwich and walks back to the hallway with Sarah and John who now follow him like hungry puppies. "Yes, Bell was a debutant once. Had a 'coming out' party and all. Quite the gal she was. Quite the gal. Of course, I was just a boy back then, but I remember."

"Why doesn't anyone know this?" Sarah asks.

"Oh, that was a long time ago. Bell's a lost soul, wandering the streets now. I think that everyone sees right through her. A ghost of the past. We're all so busy with our own lives and until we have a reason to care, we simply walk by never noticing." The Judge continues to slowly walk back toward his chambers.

"So what happened?" Sarah asks, now engrossed in the story.

"I don't know the details. That was back before you were born, Sarah. Bell's been wandering the streets for years," the Judge stops before the entrance to his chambers.

"Something had to happen," Sarah states. "I mean if she was a debutant and all. *Something* must have changed her life so drastically! That mansion's been decaying for many years."

"Yes, it has." The Judge pauses as if contemplating how much he should reveal. "Sarah, what exactly is the complaint against Bell?"

"Just that Animal Control may take Emma away if they find out that she's sleeping in the streets. Judge Joe, you know that losing her best friend would be the end of Bell." Sarah places her hand on his arm and looks at him with pleading eyes. "Doesn't she have any family? What happened to her?"

The Judge puts his hand on hers and pats it. "Slow down, young lady! I'm sure it's just a local neighbor that's concerned for Emma's well being. You know, trying to do the right thing. The truth is, it doesn't look like a stable situation! I can't say that I blame them for calling attention to it." He pauses and smiles. "I have to get back to the courtroom. Now Sarah, I know you and I don't want you worrying about this. See what you and John can find out about Bell and let me know what you come up with. If you're convinced that Emma's in safe hands, I'll do what I can to help."

Sarah looks at John. "Honey, it looks like we have some homework to do!"

"Another Christmas project?" John grins.

"It wouldn't be Christmas without Sarah saving a forlorn soul," the Judge comments.

"Thank you, Judge!" Sarah jumps up and hugs him.

"I didn't say I could perform a miracle. I'm just saying I'll help if I can. Now I have a nice, stacked meat sandwich I need to tackle before my next case. I'll see you two later." The Judge opens the door to his chambers and disappears inside.

John turns to Sarah. "The Judge seems to know a lot about Bell. He remembers her when he was a kid!"

"And she was a debutante from a wealthy family." Sarah looks off into space. "Wow, I can't even picture that. Bell Benton. Well, I'm assuming she was a Benton. I wonder what happened to the Benton family. That mansion is in ruins! Where are they? You don't think," she pauses.

"That she may still live there?" John comments. "Well, it's isolated and on acres of land. I don't suppose anyone would notice since none of the main roads go out there."

"Gosh, that's such a bizarre thought." Sarah pauses and thinks. "We need to know for sure. It should be easy enough to find out who owns that property. Let's go check out the town records tomorrow." Sarah hooks her arm in John's as they walk down the hall.

"Tomorrow's Saturday!" John looks at her and cocks his head to one side, squinting.

"Is it? Then that's perfect. We have a whole day free. We'll have time for a nice breakfast and then we can eventually mosey over to the library." Sarah smiles and pulls him closer to her side.

"But I have to pick up my Santa suit from the Mayor!" John objects.

"We have plenty of time to do that. Come on! It'll be like old times! Just you and me and . . ."

"Uh oh," John says throwing his head back.

"What?" Sarah turns her head to one side.

"Here's another Sarah holiday project!" John smirks. "And another pro bono case of yours coming. I can see it now. I might as well tell your parents that we'll be late for Christmas!" Sarah teasingly gives John a light punch in the arm. "I'm serious!" he says grabbing his arm feigning pain.

"I know you're serious. I've never been late for Christmas, so don't even think it, which means we'd better get cracking! Go take care of your case and I'll see you at the house. Don't forget that we're having company tonight," Sarah reminds him.

"Yep, I remember!" John says.

"Can you pick up a nice garlic bread? I'm making pasta," Sarah requests.

"No problem." John leans over and kisses her. "I'll see you later, Nancy Drew!"

Sarah shakes her head with a grin on her face. "Nancy Drew. Huh! I like that," she says to herself. She heads in the opposite direction and back to her office.

Chapter Three
No Moon Walk Allowed

Sarah stands in her kitchen cutting up onions as Baxter patiently sits nearby in hopes that a piece of food will make its way to the floor. She wipes tears that well up in her eyes as a result of the onion fumes. Steam seeps from the sides of a bouncing lid on a pot that is threatening to boil over. She grabs it. "Ouch!" Sarah plops the pot down on another burner and sticks her singed finger under cold water when the doorbell rings.

"Greetings!" Jessica stands at the entrance holding mistletoe over her head.

"No way!" Sarah laughs as she walks to Jessica and pulls her inside.

"It's not for you! It's for that gorgeous husband of yours!" Jessica teases.

"Give me that," Sarah says grabbing the mistletoe. "You may be my best friend, but there are limits to that! You're dangerous with that stuff."

"Dangerous, but fun!" Jessica laughs, enters the living room and removes her coat. She looks around at the comfortably decorated but chic bungalow with its wood floors and high ceilings. The large stone fireplace is ablaze; its mantle decked out with roping and lights. A tall, narrow Douglas Fir stands in the corner with twinkling white lights that reflect off of silver bulbs and glittery roping. "The place looks great, as always." Jessica walks into the dining room where a bar cart sits. "I believe it's martini time!" She picks up a martini glass and examines it.

"You know where everything's at," Sarah says, walking back into the kitchen. "I have your stuffed olives in the fridge, so get in here and join me!"

Jessica enters the kitchen with a bottle of vodka and the glass. She places both on the counter, opens the refrigerator and fumbles around.

"On the left door," Sarah instructs.

"Got it." Jessica pulls out a jar of blue cheese stuffed olives.

Sarah reaches into a cupboard, pulls a drink shaker out and hands it to Jessica. "Make it two!"

"Two? Was it a rough week?" Jessica asks bumping Sarah's hip with hers in jest.

"Not at all," Sarah answers. "In fact, we had a great week. We had a case settled out of court with full terms, and a casserole awarded to a plaintiff."

"A what?" Jessica wrinkles her forehead.

"I'll get into it later. Let's just say that Rosedale never ceases to surprise me." Sarah stirs the spaghetti sauce.

Jessica walks back to the dining room and returns with another glass then gets busy making dirty martinis. She carefully measures olive juice and vodka, pouring each over ice cubes in the shaker. "So, you're coming up on your one-year wedding anniversary! How exciting! Can you believe it? It flew by didn't it?"

"I know! So much has happened! It's been two years since Judge Joe threw us together on the Landis case." Sarah pulls out a large pot and fills it with water.

"Thank God for Mr. Landis putting that crazy Christmas tree on his roof! And thank God Judge Joe forced you two to solve the case! You might still be sneering at John!" Jessica places more ice cubes in the shaker.

"I never sneered at John!" Sarah defends.

"You most certainly did! You two were totally at odds. And look at you now! Married and running your own law firm!" Jessica shakes the martinis, making a loud clacking noise as the ice cubes jostle around the metal container. "So, what's it like working with your husband?"

"We're loving it. We really do work well together. I'm surprised." Sarah puts the small pot back on the burner and stirs the ingredients.

"Surprised?" Jessica tilts her head.

"Yeah. Well, him coming from corporate law and me coming from . . . "

"Working sad cases for free!" Jessica doesn't miss a beat.

"Not for free! And a little bit of charity never hurts. Actually, it's working out quite well. John let's me take on my 'special' cases on occasion," she smiles politely.

"Oh brother! That is one great guy you've got there. Speaking of, where is he?" Jessica continues to shake the martinis. Baxter's ears perk up and he bolts for the living room door.

"I hear martinis shaking! Is that Jessica breaking into our bar?" John teases as he enters, setting his briefcase down. He pulls his gloves and scarf off and places them on a chair next to the entrance.

"It most certainly is!" Jessica walks out of the kitchen and into the living room to greet John, giving him a big hug.

"Ohhhh, you are a good hugger!" John rocks her back and forth.

"Hey!" Sarah yells from the kitchen. "You'd better not have that mistletoe out!"

"Oh right. Your wife banned me from using the mistletoe in your house. I don't know why since I'm totally harmless!" Jessica laughs. "Don't worry, John. You're safe. Hey, shall I make it three dirty martinis?"

"Why not?" John says, pulling his coat off and hanging it in the front closet. He walks into the kitchen, placing the loaf of garlic bread on the table and grabs Sarah from behind, giving her a hug and kiss on the neck.

"Yuck!" Jessica teases, entering with the third glass. "Get a room!"

Sarah laughs. "Don't embarrass Jessica. We want our guests to be comfortable in our home."

"You mean guest," Jessica adds.

"No, she means *guests*," John says, lifting the lid to the sauce pot and looking in. He grabs a spoon and stirs the ingredients, then takes a taste.

"Uh oh," Jessica stops and stares at the two who are still busy making dinner.

"Not 'uh oh.' This is an 'uh huh!'" Sarah responds.

"This better be a really good 'uh huh,' dear girl," Jessica says as she continues to stare down Sarah. "Remember the last 'uh huh'? *That* was an 'uh *oh*' for sure, or more like an '*oh no!*'"

"Oh, Bud? He wasn't so bad! Come on! Bud's a nice guy!" John looks at Jessica as he adds salt to the pot.

"Bud wasn't so bad? He was showing us the moon walk after four beers!" Jessica adds still shaking the martini.

"I thought that was cute!" Sarah laughs. "Come on! He was adorable! I can't do the moon walk! Can you, Jessica? John, can you?"

"No, I can't do the moon walk," John smiles.

"See? Three people in this room and none of us can do the moon walk. It takes talent to do that!" Sarah grins and watches as the big pot of water begins to heat up.

"Talent and four beers." Jessica pauses and divides the martinis among the three glasses. "O.K. kids. Lay it on me. Who's the guest?"

"Rob Frost, an attorney friend of mine," John answers.

"Does he live in town? I haven't heard of him." Jessica carefully watches John's expression.

"He's the new attorney at the law firm I worked at when I first moved back to Rosedale. In fact, he's pretty much my replacement. He's a really smart guy." John says with a straight face.

"Oh boy. A smart guy. Sarah, tell John what that means." Jessica looks to Sarah for help.

"Oh, right. John, that's code for 'he's not good looking,'" Sarah responds with a smile.

"Ohhhh. Got it. Well, Jessica, you're stuck now. I guess you'll just have to find out for yourself. Besides, it's not a date. Just four friends getting together for dinner. No obligations whatsoever." John places the lid on the pot. "The sauce is perfect, hon."

"Don't think I didn't see you tampering with it." Sarah smirks at John and takes a handful of pasta into her hands, placing it into the now bubbling water in the larger pot.

Jessica places two stuffed olives in each martini and hands John and Sarah each a glass. "Here's to 'uh oh' or whatever walks through that door!" They raise their glasses and toast.

"Cheers!" John takes a sip and puts his glass down, before pulling out plates and silverware.

"Just a few minutes and we'll be ready." Sarah unwraps the bread, slices and butters it, adding rosemary before placing it on a sheet of foil in the oven.

The doorbell soon rings and John walks to the entrance, sighs in anticipation of Jessica's reaction and opens it. "Come in, my friend!" A tall man steps in and smacks John's hand in a friendly handshake. "Rob, it's good to have you here. Let me take your coat." Baxter nudges Rob who quickly greets the dog, giving his head a rub.

"Hey there, handsome guy!" Baxter's tail wags wildly.

"That's Baxter," John announces. "So how's everything at the firm?"

"Going great! Taking on some interesting cases," Rob shares.

"Glad to hear it. Come on. Let's join the ladies." John hangs up Rob's coat before the two walk through the dining room and into the kitchen.

"Rob, I'd like you to meet Sarah's best friend, Jessica. Jessica? This is Rob." John smiles and walks to the wine fridge.

"I, I . . . it's a pleasure," Jessica stutters, looking noticeably shaken. Sarah snickers.

"Jessica, the pleasure's mine," Rob says, extending his hand.

Sarah steps over to Rob and kisses his cheek. "Welcome, stranger. I'm so glad you could make it!"

"Sarah, you're looking lovely as always," Rob smiles.

John pulls out a bottle of burgundy wine and shows it to Rob. "Your favorite, Sir," he says, placing a wine glass on the counter. Rob walks over to John and looks at the bottle.

"You didn't! John, this is outstanding. An excellent year, too. Thank you. What a thoughtful gesture!" Rob reveals a big, gleaming smile and Jessica could swear that his eyes twinkled.

"Yes, Rob *loves* a good burgundy," Sarah says giving Jessica a wink. "Rob, can you do the moon walk?"

"I'm sorry? Did you say 'moon walk?' Why? Does someone want to know how to moon walk? I'm the wrong guy," Rob says, examining the label on the wine bottle. "I'll leave that to Michael Jackson," he smiles. Jessica gives Sarah a wide eyed look of disapproval, but says nothing.

"Here you go, my friend." Rob hands the bottle back to John who pulls out a corkscrew and winds it tightly into the cork, pushing down on the levers until it pops. "So, Jessica, I hear that you have your own business?" Rob asks.

"Yes," Jessica responds, starting to blush. She pulls at her turtleneck to hide the red blotches that are creeping up her neck and toward her cheeks. "I was working for a big employer, but now I own a technology consulting business. It's just me, but I enjoy it."

"Nothing wrong with 'just you,'" Rob responds, taking the glass of wine that John hands him. He swirls the wine and gives it a long sniff before taking a sip. "Ah, beautiful!" Rob clinks John's martini glass. "Cheers, my friend!"

"Uh, cheers!" Jessica nervously blurts out and leans across the room to clink their glasses. John gives a quiet snicker.

"So, Rob, I hear that you work at John's former law firm?" Jessica acts like a happy school girl.

"Yes. I've been here in Rosedale a few months now. When John left, they decided to recruit and thanks to John's recommendation, I was considered. And, well, here I am!" He lifts his glass again.

THE MIRACLE SERIES

"Very nice," Jessica does the same. "And you like Rosedale?"

"I transferred from Arizona, so it's quite a change with the cold coming on. But, yes, I think it's a quaint and interesting town. Everyone has been so friendly too." He examines Jessica's face.

Jessica looks at Rob's handsome features. His straight nose, big smile, thick hair, and fit physique. "Oh, it's usually not this cold," Jessica says feeling self conscious. She turns to Sarah. "Sarah, may we take some items into the dining room for you?" she says fidgeting with her hair.

"Certainly. Why don't you and Rob get seated. Jessica, if you can take these napkins in, I'd appreciate it. Rob, just take the wine, we'll be all set," Sarah directs the two.

"I think we did O.K.," John whispers to Sarah as Jessica and Rob make their way into the dining room.

"I think we did more than O.K.!" Sarah responds. "Go ahead and drain the pasta and I'll get the sauce and bread ready. Sarah places the steaming garlic bread in a basket and covers it with a cloth napkin. The smell of garlic and basil fill the room. She pours the thick, red pasta sauce into a tureen and carries it into the dining room, placing it on the table. John brings in a steaming, large bowl heaped with spaghetti and they take their seats.

"So, Rob, what do you do in your spare time, *if* you have any?" Sarah asks.

"This may sound crazy coming from a busy attorney, but I actually love renovating homes. I renovated several in Arizona and there are quite a few fixer uppers in this town that I'd love to get my hands on." The friends pass the pasta and sauce around, filling their plates.

"That is *so* interesting!" Jessica turns to Rob and places her elbows on the table, resting her chin on her hands, staring intently at him. "Have you purchased anything yet?"

"No, I haven't quite found the right one, but I've been looking," he smiles. "So, Jessica," Rob spins pasta on his fork, "is that a bit of Irish that gives you those beautiful green eyes and auburn hair?" Jessica bats her eyelashes and laughs nervously.

Sarah turns to John and rolls her eyes. They both hide a smile.

"Oh, a bit on my Mom's side going way back," she leans toward him and tilts her head to the side, flipping her hair and smiling.

"I see. Very nice. So, what do you do with *your* free time?" Rob continues, glancing up as he puts the forkful of pasta in his mouth.

Jessica picks at her plate, careful not to make a mess as she eats. "Biking, hiking, and this is going to sound crazy, but," she pauses.

"Go ahead, Jessica, say it," Sarah prods. "She likes to skeet shoot."

"And she's really good at it," John adds.

"But I want to specify that I only shoot skeets," Jessica giggles. "You know, clay pigeons. Nothing that breaths!"

"So far," John teases.

"Yeah make sure you stay on her good side!" Sarah grins. "She's a good shot."

"I think that's awesome!" Rob says. "I *love* skeet shooting! Do you shoot at the Trenton Lake Shooting Club?"

"Yes! Do you belong?" Jessica asks, her voice getting higher.

"I do," Rob lifts his wine glass and clinks hers. "I think we need to go shooting some time soon. And, I don't hunt, either. Clay pigeons only for me. I'm a nature lover."

"Well then we need to go on a hike some time up in the Blue Ridge. There are some great trails," Jessica adds. "Have you had a chance to explore the mountains?"

"Coming from Arizona, hiking in mountains isn't something I've done much of. It would be great to explore the Blue Ridge. I haven't been up there yet. It just seemed odd to go alone," Rob shares.

"Oh, I go up there all of the time! I'll show you around and you'll be totally comfortable exploring on your own," Jessica adds.

"Well, now that I have you, I won't have to go alone," Rob gives her a flirtatious look.

John leans over to Sarah. "Our work here is done," he whispers in her ear. Sarah gives him a nod and raised eyebrow.

The four chat and share stories over the course of the dinner. The fire continues to crackle and lights up the living room, eventually dying down as the hours pass. The Christmas tree twinkles, the evening progresses, and eventually the friends decide to call it a night.

Rob and Jessica assist in cleaning the table, walking plates into the kitchen. "Jessica, may I escort you home?" Rob asks.

"Why yes! That would be really nice. I walked here. I live just a couple of blocks down the road and I'd love some company!" Jessica replies.

"I walked here too!" Rob announces. The two can't take their eyes off of one another.

The friends finish bringing in the last of the items and John and Sarah escort the couple to the door.

"Sarah, John, thank you so much for a wonderful night!" Rob hugs them both, as does Jessica.

"Thank you *so* much! The dinner was fabulous," Jessica winks at Sarah.

John and Sarah, escort them onto the porch and wave as they watch the couple hook arms and walk down the sidewalk on their way home.

"What do you think?" John says, putting his arm around Sarah.

"A pretty good match I'd say," Sarah gives John a nudge. "Come on. Let's finish cleaning up the kitchen and hit the sack. We have research in the morning!"

"Oh, right! The girl doesn't forget anything!" John laughs and looks down at Baxter. "Come on Baxter, it's time for bed! We have a mystery to solve tomorrow!" Baxter licks John's hand and the three walk back into the house.

Chapter Four
Ghosts of the Past

John and Sarah make their way up the steps of the Rosedale library, a brown brick, three story building covered with ivy. Its gabled roof is adorned with cement scrolls and gargoyles that guard the entrance. They head straight to the information desk where an elderly lady graciously refers them to the archives section; a small room with glass windows that reveal shelves stuffed with old, faded books.

"Not everything's been transferred to digital, I'm afraid," the librarian shares. "You may have to research the old fashioned way and pull out books and some film slides. The viewer's over here." She points to the corner of the room. "Others are available in our online archive. It depends on the importance of the publication and how old it is. I don't need to tell you that there are going to be a lot of Rosedale articles and announcements that haven't make the cut for an upgrade yet. You'll need to get creative, and just holler if you can't find something. I'll be here all day."

"Thanks, Mrs. Miller. We appreciate you showing us where to find some of the older local documents." The two make their way to the small room and examine the many, packed shelves. Sarah seats herself at a long, wood table. A musty odor fills the room; a result of years of collections and donated records that were stuck away in old homes and basements, rarely touched.

"You can start here. Feel free to access whatever you need," Mrs. Miller says as she enters the room and walks to a shelf. She pulls out an overly large book with darkened, yellowed pages and places it in front of Sarah.

"Good luck!" Mrs. Miller leaves the couple alone to explore.

"What do you think?" Sarah asks John. "We start with the Benton family records?"

"Yeah, I think that's the only place to look right now. I know you're as curious as I am. Let's find out who Bell really is." John joins Sarah and one by one, they scour through books and archived articles.

John leans in closer to Sarah, keeping his voice low. "Why do I get the feeling that Judge Joe knows more than he's sharing?"

"Funny, but I had that same feeling." Sarah stares at him. "Do you think we should have pressed him for more?"

"You know the Judge. He operates at his own pace, and his own rules. I just felt like he didn't quite want to reveal details." John continues to run his finger down faded, fragile pages.

"Yeah, I sensed that too. Maybe he thinks that we're interfering. I mean, Bell keeps to herself, put aside your weekly pot pie lunches," Sarah laughs.

"Right. Well, maybe we *are* interfering. I mean here we are on a Saturday morning nosing into someone's life when no one has asked for our help. Maybe we should just leave things as they are." John looks up at Sarah, waiting for her answer.

"It's an option, but, wouldn't it be tragic if Emma got picked up by the animal shelter? Once that happens, there will be no turning back and you know that Bell certainly has no chance of fighting that battle." Sarah pauses and thinks. "No, John. We need to do this. We're only looking into what is already public information."

John gives Sarah a thoughtful look. "You're right. I guess this isn't prying. Just gathering facts, right?"

"Exactly. We need to know what the situation is if we're going to be of any help. Now let's get what we can and I promise we'll spend some fun time together today," Sarah responds, putting out her hand for a shake.

"O.K. deal." John shakes her hand and they get back to their research.

It doesn't take long before John finds something. "Wow, Sarah, here's Bell's birth information." John turns the book around for Sarah to look at.

"Bellissima Maria Benton! That has to be her. What a pretty name. So, Bell is Bellissima. Look! Born August 4th, 1941 to Antonio Marcos and Maria Santos Benton. It says that she was born at home in the Benton mansion!"

"That's amazing," Sarah responds, leaning over to take a closer look. She stares at it for a few minutes and then turns back to the viewer. "So she *was* born in that mansion and she is indeed a Benton. Now we have some dates to work with."

They dig back into their sources when Sarah comes upon an article. "Wait, wait, wait! Get over here." She moves over for John to take a look. "Here it is! The Debutante Ball of Rosedale. Here's an article and a picture of Belle! She was so young. Oh, John, look at this!" Sarah pulls John over to look into the viewer.

"Oh my gosh, that's amazing!" John looks at the picture in disbelief. "Judge Joe is right. She's beautiful! I wouldn't have been able to pick her out, sad to say."

"I know. And look at her Dad, presenting her! I think that's her Mom there in the background." The two stare at the picture in amazement.

"So, now what?" John looks at Sarah.

"We fill in the blanks between then and now." Sarah turns back to the books, overwhelmed at where to begin.

"Sarah, that's a big blank to fill in. What happens when we get all of this information? It doesn't help us with her present situation. Even if we can find out where she lives, the fact is that she seems to be emotionally unstable and wanders the streets." John places his hand on Sarah's shoulder.

"Maybe, maybe not. I know it sounds impossible, but there has to be something here. A person doesn't come from that kind of background and just end up on the streets. There has to be a missing piece.

After all, she was an accepted woman of high society. A debutante, with a Mom and a Dad in what was once the most beautiful home in the county. You didn't grow up here, but I remember when that mansion was something to look at."

"What do you remember about it? About the family?" John asks.

"Well, I knew the Benton family lived there at one time, but no one seemed to know them. That mansion sits on the outskirts, far from any interaction with the town residents. We never saw anyone coming or going. It just slowly decayed. I suppose her parents had passed long before I could remember."

"Sarah, let's see who owns the Benton house." John locates property records and slowly scans through each page and address. "Take a look. That mansion is still listed under the Benton estate, but I can't tell who has control of it. For all we know, there's a relative or attorney somewhere that's in charge."

"If so, why wouldn't Bell be under better care? And just because it's in the Benton name doesn't means that Bell has access to it," Sarah responds.

"Sarah, we need to remember that if someone is of sound mind then they have free will to live the life they choose," John reminds her. "And even if she owns it, it doesn't prove that she chooses to live there. Maybe she lives at the retirement home nearby."

"Not likely. I don't think that they would allow her to wander the streets." Sarah looks at her viewing screen. "That would be easy enough to check out."

The two log on to a computer stationed nearby and begin to search Bell's address. "John, it looks like the Benton property is the only address Bell is associated with. It's difficult to imagine that one person could live in such a huge place that's falling apart."

John sorts through more records. "Sarah, look. Here are the death records for her parents. Both of them died within a short period of each other, many years ago."

"Oh, that is so sad. She's all alone. There are no siblings recorded, either. John, I'll bet that's when the mansion went into decay."

"We're going to have to do a lot more research, Sarah. I'm not sure where to start." John and Sarah look at each other in silence.

"You know what we need to do, don't you?" Sarah raises an eyebrow.

"Yeah, I do. It's the only way to find out. We need to go out there." John pauses. "The challenge is that if she does live there, there's a good chance that she won't answer the door. We may not know for sure."

"I know, but certainly we'd be able to tell if someone has been there. We'll have to be very careful, and I don't want to trespass. It won't be easy. It's sitting out there on its own with not much surrounding it. A car and two people snooping would be pretty noticeable." Sarah points out.

"You're right. We'll have to be discrete. But there's one thing we're not thinking about," John states. "If we find out she inhabits the place, then what? What does that prove except that she isn't sleeping on the streets? I'm not sure it will help save Emma from being removed."

"You're right." Sarah looks off into the distance, deep in thought.

John watches Sarah as the wheels turn in her mind. "Sarah, this is much more than just Emma, isn't it?" Sarah looks at him with puppy eyes. "I know that look. We're doing way too much research just to find out where Bell lives or what conditions Emma lives under. You're just a born sleuth and you aren't going to stop until you know everything about her are you?" Sarah gives a proud smile. "Yeah, that's what I thought," John shakes his head. "Sleuth combined with the 'Sarah save a soul at Christmas club' translates into a lot of work."

Sarah leans forward and grabs John's arm. "John, this is going to be really 'out there,' but,"

John interrupts. "Oh Sarah, nothing that you say will shock me. I've heard it all from you, dear! Go ahead. I'll brace myself."

"Oh stop!" she pushes his arm. "I was wondering if we shouldn't just talk to her and offer our help. I mean, then we wouldn't be sneaking around. She most likely doesn't even know that she could lose Emma. If we told her about the situation, she may be more likely to open up to us. Then we can represent her if we needed to, and it would be . . ."

"Pro bono, of course." John finishes her sentence and smiles. "Yes, Sarah, I already knew we were going down that road. Hey, I don't disagree. If you think that's the best way to reach her, then you have my support." He pauses. "Perhaps only one of us should speak with her. Maybe she'd respond better to a woman. She doesn't say anything to me. I have the feeling that you would be much better at this."

"You mean that? You're O.K. if we approach her?" Sarah asks.

"Of course. Let's handle Bell like we would anyone else. Look at Mr. Landis. He wouldn't accept your help and it worked out alright. At least Bell can make up her own mind if she wants us to intervene."

"*If* she has her own mind," Sarah reminds him. "You're assuming she *is* of sound mind."

"Come on. Let's pack up here for now. We can look up mental health and medical records on Bell during our next trip. I need to get to the Mayor's office to pick up my Santa suit for the big tree lighting event. I want to get it to the cleaners and make sure it still fits for my big night!"

"O.K. But, I think it's time to go back to Judge Joe and press for more information. If we can get more out of him, we may not have to spend time researching this," Sarah declares.

"I think you're right. Come one, let's enjoy the rest of our day." Sarah and John gather their coats and head to the Mayor's house.

Sarah slowly walks up the dirt road leading to the mansion. She stops and stares at it. There isn't a sound except for the whistle of a slight, cold breeze. She wonders what stories it could tell. The events, births, deaths, and memories imprinted in its walls are all a secret now. The once glorious home has no one to tell its history of challenges, triumphs, joy, and sorrow.

The southern mansion no longer boasts strong, two-story columns. They are now weathered and weak, paint peeling, barely holding the weight of the roof. The tall windows are now dim and dirty, faintly revealing dingy curtains made of the finest fabric, now faded and disintegrating. Sarah approaches the home, slowly navigating up the brick walkway, now dirt covered. Flower beds that once displayed impeccable landscaping are now home to tall weeds and layers of dead leaves and plants.

Sarah cautiously walks onto the massive porch, careful not to fall through the rotted planks that creak and threaten to buckle underneath her. She stops and stands in silence, taking a deep breath in preparation of the task she has committed to. She stares at the weathered door when a bird tweets, watching her from a tree overhead. Sarah looks up and smiles, then takes another deep breath.

She steps forward when out of the corner of her eye she catches a movement from inside. Fear rushes through her and her body freezes until she convinces herself that it must simply be an animal. Certainly no one could live in this uninhabitable place, or does a ghostly specter roam the halls? Sarah's breathing increases as she anticipates what might transpire. It was time to do what she came here for. She steps forward, her hands trembling and raises the metal knocker. Embellished with a deeply tarnished lion head, it angrily stares back at her as if warning her not to proceed. Sarah releases it and the metal clash reverberates and echoes against the wood and hollow interior. Was it her imagination or was there indeed someone or something lurking inside? There is only silence. She raises the knocker twice more. Again, silence. Sarah takes a deep breath and then sighs with relief. Perhaps it was an animal after all.

Sarah turns and carefully navigates her way off of the rotted porch when she hears something. Footsteps? They draw nearer, getting louder, and then stop. She turns to look at the towering door and sees the handle slowly turn. Her blood freezes in her veins. The door creaks open in slow motion. Sarah can barely breath.

There, in front of her stands a slender young woman, dressed in a flowing, white long gown adorned with flower appliques. Her light brown hair is pulled up on her head and intricately weaved into an elegant pattern. A bright white flower is tucked in the left side of the upsweep.

The young woman smiles. "Come in." She swings the door wide open, sweeping her arm out to show Sarah the way.

"Oh, I don't want to intrude. I was just, I was just," Sarah sees that the young woman is not listening to her. "I passed by and, and I was looking for. . ."

The woman slowly walks toward two wooden pocket doors to the left of the large foyer and turns toward Sarah who stands at the entrance, peeking in. She motions for Sarah to follow and giggles as she turns and places her hands on the handles of the solid, heavy doors and slides them apart.

Sarah cautiously steps into the elegant foyer, appointed with rich carpets. She is amazed that the decaying home's interior is totally intact and maintained. She looks to her left, where the young woman disappeared and slowly walks to the opening of the room where the sound of music, chatter and laughter spills out. She steps inside and is in disbelief at the opulence that is revealed. Impeccable turn-of-the-century furnishings adorn the room which is brightly lit by a massive, glistening crystal chandelier. Young couples stand in groups, deep in conversation, and dressed perfectly in formal attire. The women in their best gowns, hair up and curled, pinned and secured with jeweled combs are all wearing long, white gloves. The guests are holding glass cups like those used with punch bowls, enjoying the music of a string quartet situated in the corner of the room. The men are dressed in tuxedo suits with long tails. Several older couples are among the attendees, yet no one acknowledges Sarah's presence.

Sarah steps further in and looks around for the young woman who greeted her. She spots her on the other side of the room, now laughing and chatting with a young man. Sarah discretely walks toward her sliding against the wall as if scaling the edge of a high building, hoping that she will not be noticed. Still, no one seems interested in the underdressed newcomer.

"Hello." Sarah carefully steps up to the woman and gentleman, trying not to interrupt the conversation. "Hi, I'm Sarah Rivera. I didn't mean to intrude. I was just wondering if anyone lived here. Or I mean, I was wondering who used to live here, or uh, who lives here now. I'm actually looking for someone by the name of Bell. Do you know her? I'm really not supposed to be here."

The young woman stops and stares at Sarah with a kind expression. Her perfect skin shines and her big brown eyes framed with long, thick lashes express complete joy. She smiles and the young gentleman next to her speaks. "Of course you're supposed to be here. Let me introduce myself. I am Prescott."

"Oh, O.K. Prescott," Sarah extends her hand. "It's a pleasure to meet you. I'm Sarah."

"I know," the young man says with a smile. He extends his hand and instead of a shake, he takes her hand in his and kisses the top of it.

"Oh! O.K.," Sarah feels awkward at the gesture. "You know me? Have we met?" She examines his face, hoping to find familiarity. Prescott sports a thick mustache, and wavy hair parted in the middle. Was this a costume party? Sarah is confused. She begins to ask a question when the music changes to a melodic dance tune and all of the guests turn their attention toward the couple.

Prescott stretches his hand out toward the beautiful woman, their eyes never losing contact. Sarah is confused and feels awkward, wanting to run out the door. But something tells her not to. The young woman smiles at him and takes his hand. He escorts her to the middle of the floor and they begin to dance a beautiful, flowing waltz. Her dress billows out as he twirls her around the room. They float in unison, dancing as all watch, their faces full of love and joy. It is a magical scene that captures the attention of everyone, now fixated on them.

Suddenly, the room becomes blurred and hazy. Sarah shakes her head, trying to clear the fuzzy feeling. Prescott seems distance, almost transparent.

"Wait!" Sarah yells. "Come back! Wait! I need to ask you something! Prescott!"

Prescott never loses his attention on the beautiful woman. She too, begins to disappear and the entire room becomes a white mist. "Prescott! Prescott!" Sarah tries to move toward them, but her body is frozen; paralyzed.

John grabs Sarah by her shoulders. "Sarah! Wake up! Honey, wake up!" Sarah opens her eyes to see John's face in front of hers.

"Prescott?" she says, staring blankly at him.

"Prescott? We're coming up on our one-year anniversary and you're already dreaming about other men? Great!" John gives her a sweet grin.

"No, I mean Prescott, the man who introduced himself to me. He kissed my hand and was dancing with the beautiful woman. It was a party, with gowns and tuxedos, oh, and a stringed quartet! It was beautiful, but then she disappeared! They all disappeared!"

"Who disappeared? Who's she? May we back up a minute here? What are you talking about?" John props his head on his hand as he lays on his side.

"The mansion. I was at the mansion. You know, the Benton place, and a beautiful young woman invited me in. It was a party with dozens of lovely, young couples socializing with one another." She pauses and rubs her eyes then sits up. "You know the dresses that we saw in the debutante pictures? They were dressed like that. And the men, they had those long tail tuxedos on. The women wore those long, white gloves too! The exterior was terrible and decayed, but the interior was beautiful with a large crystal chandelier, and expensive carpets, and that old fashioned kind of furniture from the early 1900's."

"Wow, you're really obsessed with that Bell story." John lays his head back on his pillow.

"John, it was real." She stares into the dark room. "Prescott."

"Yeah, who's Prescott?" He turns his head to look at Sarah.

"I don't know, but Prescott introduced himself to me. They were dancing and everyone was watching. They were obviously so much in love." She is silent then turns to John. "John, it was so real! Do you think that the dream was a message? Do you think that someone is trying to communicate something important?"

"O.K., now you're getting really strange on me. Sarah, obviously you took all of the things we were just looking at in those newspapers and created a story. It's just a jumble of information floating around in your head."

"I don't know, John. There was something about it all." Sarah slides back down and pulls the covers up over her shoulders. She turns and looks at him as their heads rest on their pillows. "I know you're right. It just seemed so real."

"Sarah, I know you're concerned. We'll get to the bottom of this. I think the attorney in you is bent on finding all of the facts. That and your soft heart." John puts his arm around her and pulls her close. "Honey, get some sleep and I promise you we'll find out more about your Bell. No one's taking little Emma away, so get some shut eye, O.K.?"

"Yeah, you're right. I know I sound crazy right now, but it was just so *real*!" Sarah cuddles with John and pulls the blankets up around their shoulders. John quickly dozes off while Sarah continues to stare into the dark room hoping that she can somehow slip back to sleep and into the dimension that she left when she suddenly sees a flash of light. And again. She sits up and looks at the side table next to her. There, sparkling in the dark is the Christmas star that Mr. Landis returned. It flashes yet again and a peace comes over her. She smiles and soon drifts into a sound slumber.

Chapter Five
Hot Mulled Wine and a Secret or Two

"Hello, I'm Sarah Rivera, the person who phoned earlier about Emma." Sarah steps up to the counter just inside the entrance of the Oak County Animal Control building.

"Oh yes, Mrs. Rivera. Our Director, Carol Winslow is expecting you. Please take a seat and I'll let her know that you're here." The woman behind the counter leaves and walks down a hallway and through an office door. Sarah patiently waits.

Soon, Carol Winslow appears. "Mrs. Rivera? Please come back to my office."

"Oh, please call me Sarah." Sarah extends her hand as does Carol.

"Of course. And please call me Carol. I understand that you're here to inquire about the dog Emma. Are you representing her owner?"

"Oh, gosh no." Sarah thinks. "Well, at least not at the moment. Does she need representation?"

"Oh no. As of today, we're only looking into the situation. We don't just yank pets from their owners unless we have solid grounds to do so. I understand that Bell is, or appears to be, homeless."

"That hasn't been determined. I've actually been doing some research myself." Carol leads Sarah to her office where they take a seat. Sarah sighs and leans forward, placing her arms on Carol's desk.

"Carol, I'm a real animal lover. But I also have a soft spot in my heart for disadvantaged people." Sarah rethinks her statement. "Let's just say I have a concern for people that society may not fully understand or are unable to handle such situations themselves, and Bell is definitely in that category. I don't need to tell you that she's been a Rosedale 'character' for years. No one has ever questioned the safety of her dog, and Emma seems to be a healthy and happy animal. I'm not sure what the issue is. Granted, Bell's health is more questionable than Emma's considering her age. But, Carol, we just don't know. I'm here because I don't believe that Emma is in any danger or risk. I would like to ask that you not make any decisions until I have the opportunity to investigate this further. I'm willing to put in the time and I'll work with you to make sure that you can come to an accurate conclusion. And, yes, if at some point Bell needs representation, I will gladly supply those services." Sarah pauses and takes a breath. "Carol, I'm really hoping it doesn't get to that point."

Carol leans forward and touches Sarah's hand. "Sarah, I'm more than happy to work with you. I promise you that nothing is going to happen unless we find that there's a sound reason to remove Emma. My concern is the cold temperatures. I can't make a promise as to the results, but I can promise you that I will be fair. The complaint that we received is a valid one and we need to give it serious consideration. I'm sure you understand that."

Sarah gives Carol a smile. "Carol, I completely understand, but I can't shake the feeling that there's another story here that we don't know."

Carol stands. "My hope is that it's a good one. Sarah, you have my word that I will be in communication with any updates. I'm responsible for giving this complaint serious attention, so I appreciate any insights that you can share."

Sarah stands. "Carol, thank you so much for meeting with me. You have my phone number, so if there are any developments, please call. I hope that this results in a happy ending for everyone." They shake hands.

"I certainly hope so, too. Sarah, thank you for coming by." Carol walks Sarah to the entrance and bids her farewell. Sarah makes her way to the parking lot and looks back at the building. A sadness comes over her. The situation just became very real and for the first time, in a very long time, Sarah feels powerless. She gets into her car and slowly pulls out of the parking lot and back to downtown Rosedale.

As she nears the center of town Sarah sees a familiar sight. "Oh my gosh!" she gasps. There, in the distance walking on a side street is Bell and Emma. Sarah quickly turns down the street, driving slowly until she nears the pair. She pulls the car to the curb and parks it, quietly observing.

"What do I do?" she says out loud. "O.K., I can do this. I can do this!" Sarah exits the car and makes her way toward them. "I just need to be gentle. Just be non-threatening," she whispers to herself. She quickens her pace, nearing the pair when Bell becomes aware that she is being followed. Bell speeds up, glancing back and shuffling as fast as she can as Sarah keeps up with her.

"Bell! It's Sarah Rivera! I just want to chat with you for a moment!" Sarah shouts and begins to catch up. Bell continues to walk faster, struggling to escape as Sarah approaches. She suddenly ducks into a small pathway between two homes as Emma runs by her side.

"Bell, I just want to ask you a question. I don't mean any harm!" Sarah shouts, then stops and watches, realizing that her efforts are in vain. "I only wanted to. . ." Sarah quietly says as she stands in the snow watching. "I just wanted to talk."

Bell continues to shuffle as fast as she can, glancing back, with Emma close at her feet. They make it to the end of the path where they disappear behind the home. Sarah continues to stare.

"Real smart, Sarah. Real smart," Sarah mumbles to herself. She returns to her car and drives back to her home.

"Bark!"

"What? You want to wear the elf hat?" John looks at Baxter closely.

"Bark! Bark!"

"Yes? O.K. Come here Baxter." The dog walks to John. "Sit!"

Baxter sits. "O.K. Bax, here you go." John puts an elf hat on Baxter who looks content.

"Bark! Bark!"

"Oh John! You aren't putting that hat on Baxter now! Get that off of him!" Sarah says as she enters the living room. There sits Baxter in front of John who, dressed as Santa, is seated on the sofa.

"What? Look at him! He likes it! The annual tree lighting is the event of the year. Baxter and I need to look our best!" John grabs Baxter and gives him a back rub. The dog looks as though he is smiling.

"Lord, help me!" Sarah shakes her head. She sits down on the sofa next to John and gives a big sigh.

"Sarah, you shouldn't have chased her!" John continues to pet Baxter.

"I didn't really chase her. I was just trying to catch up with her. You know, she's not as slow as everyone thinks she is!" Sarah replies.

"Well, I doubt you're going to get a second chance. It looks like I'll have to approach her the next time I see her at '*The Pot Hole*,' if she'll even trust me now. It's not likely that I'll have any more luck than you did. Frankly, I don't even know how to approach her." John takes a bright red sweater and places it over Baxter's head then slips his front legs through the arms.

"Oh John, really?" Sarah sees that the sweater has a Santa face on it.

"You're right. I should have put the sweater on before I put on his hat. It's cute, don't you think? I don't want anyone to question that this is Santa's dog, I mean elf!" Baxter barks. "See? Baxter agrees."

"Baxter barked because his leash is on and he thinks he's going for a walk! I can't even think about what we're going to do about Bell right now. I'm kicking myself. Come on, Santa, my parents are going to be there soon along with Jessica and Rob."

Sarah is dressed in leggings and tall boots, a leather jacket and black knit cap.

"What is this? Mrs. Claus dressed in black? You look more like a winter Ninja!" John examines Sarah.

"A warm winter Ninja!" Sarah protests. "No one cares about me. They'll be lined up to see you and Baxter. Besides, I'm only Mrs. Claus to you. Otherwise, I'm just another person in the crowd. I'll be keeping my parents and Jessica company, thank you."

"Well, Baxter and I are ready." John stands and pats his stomach. "Do I need more padding?" He sticks his stomach out for Sarah to examine.

"Let's just say that you're a healthy Santa. You look fine." Sarah pokes at John's belly.

"Healthy. Hmmm. O.K. I'm good with that." John grabs Baxter's leash.

Sarah opens the door for them. Baxter bolts, dragging John behind him. Sarah locks the door and catches up with them. "Slow down you two!" she laughs.

The three briskly walk several blocks to the town square where a massive, tall tree stands in the center median. The streets are blocked from traffic and are bustling with families, vendors, and children that run and dodge the crowds. Musicians play holiday music and carolers sing their cheery tunes, dressed in turn of the century attire. The tree, loaded with ornaments sparkles in the darkness as it awaits the big switch to be flipped and illuminate the square. The walkways are lined with lamp posts decorated with white and red twinkling lights and storefronts display their holiday best.

"Good luck, Santa!" Sarah tugs on John's Santa beard. "And Baxter, make Santa behave!" The dog wags his tail and jumps up, giving Sarah a lick on the face.

"Send your parents and everyone my love! I'll be tied up for the rest of the night with the kids after the ceremony. Santa takes requests from all kiddies, if you care to visit!" John raises his eyebrows.

"I'll give it serious consideration!" Sarah smiles. "Bye Santa! I'll see you and your elf back at the North Pole!" The three part. Sarah makes her way through the noisy crowd and quickly spots her parents. She greets them with hugs and kisses.

"Hey Mom and Dad!" Next to them is their neighbor, Mrs. Costello, an elderly lady in a wheelchair, draped in a red plaid blanket, wearing a Santa hat. "Mrs. Costello! I hope you're warm enough out here! You look festive as always!" Sarah gives Mrs. Costello a kiss on her cheek.

"She insisted on her Santa hat as always," Sarah's Mom shares.

"When you get to be my age, you really don't care about how silly you look! It keeps my head warm!" Mrs. Costello declares. "Where is your young man?'

"Speaking of looking silly, John's playing Santa again this year and poor Baxter is decked out with a hat and sweater. He and Baxter had to go straight to Santa's post, so he's going to be tied up granting wishes all night." Sarah answers.

"Well, we need more men here! Too many women!" Mrs. Costello announces.

"I think that will be rectified shortly," Sarah says, looking around.

"Oh?" Mrs. Wright says with an inquisitive expression.

"Yeah, Jessica has a new beau. They seem to get along quite well!" Sarah continues to survey the crowd.

"Jessica? Oh that is so nice! Who is the young man?" Mrs. Wright asks.

"An attorney that recently moved to Rosedale. A friend of John's. He's a really nice guy," Sarah shares.

"Jessica? Our Jessica has a boyfriend? It's about time!" Mr. Wright teases.

"Jim, don't you embarrass that girl when she gets here," Mrs. Wright orders.

"Jessica can take a good teasing!" Mr. Wright gives his wife a look of confidence.

"Oh! Hey! Jessica!" Sarah shouts. "There she is now! Jessica! Over here!" Jessica spots her, waves and heads toward Sarah and her

A BELL FOR CHRISTMAS

parents. She is wearing a fashionable white parka with a faux fur hood and matching mittens, black leggings and faux fur boots.

"Here you are! How are you? Mr. and Mrs. Wright, it's good to see you!" Jessica hugs them both and leans close to Sarah. "Guess who's joining us?"

"I was hoping he would! Mr. Frost I presume?" Sarah is pleased.

"Yes! He'll be here in a minute. He's getting us hot chocolate. Sarah, he's fabulous!" Jessica puts her face in her mittens. "Oh my gosh! He's wonderful!"

"First of all, wow, look at you! You look like you walked off the page of a fashion magazine. You're adorable and you're glowing! Jessica, I don't think I've ever seen you like this! My guess is that it's going well?" Sarah smiles at Jessica who is beaming.

"I might as well just say it. I'm in love! He's perfect, Sarah." Jessica speaks softly, so that the others won't hear. "Is it that obvious? Did I overdo the outfit? I don't want to look like I'm trying too hard! Am I acting like a fool?"

"Obvious? Don't bother whispering. I think that everyone here can see that you're 'head over heels' girl! Don't worry about it! You look great, and you are not acting like a fool! You're in love!" Sarah puts her arms around Jessica. "I'm so happy for you!"

"It's about time," Jessica says, giving Sarah a hug. "Thank you for not giving up on me!"

"Are you kidding? You're my best friend in the world. I always knew that there was someone out there as incredible as you!" Sarah looks at Jessica with a big smile.

"You're the best." Jessica kisses her cheek and looks over Sarah's shoulder. "Oh, here he comes. Rob! Over here!"

Rob spots the women and walks to the group, carrying a cardboard tray filled with cups of hot chocolate. "Hello everyone! Hot chocolate to warm you up!" Rob leans over and gives Jessica a kiss. She giggles and blushes. Sarah gives her a grin and smiles.

"Rob, these are Sarah's parents, Mr. and Mrs. Wright. This is my, this is Rob," Jessica stumbles with her words.

Rob shakes Mr. Wright's hand. "I'm Jessica's boyfriend." He looks at Jessica. "You can say it, dear," he teases. Jessica nervously laughs.

"Rob, this is my parents' neighbor, Mrs. Costello," Sarah says. Rob shakes her hand.

"So glad to meet you! Aren't you a nice young man, and so tall!" Mrs. Costello says.

"Rob, welcome to the team! You've got your hands full with this one." Mr. Wright grabs Jessica and squeezes her shoulders.

"Mr. Wright!" She frowns.

"Oh, I mean it in the best possible way, Jessica. Brains and beauty is a dangerous combination!" He wraps both arms around her shoulders and rocks her back and forth.

"You charmer!" she teases.

"While you two are flattering each other, I'm going to drink some of this hot chocolate before it gets cold!" Sarah takes a cup. "Thank you, Rob."

Rob hands out the rest of the cups. "Mrs. Wright?"

"Thank you, Rob. That was so thoughtful," Mrs. Wright takes the cup and rubs the sides to warm up. Rob hands a cup to Mrs. Costello.

"Oh, thank you dear! What a handsome young man you are!" Mrs. Costello takes the hot chocolate and gives him a flirtatious look. Rob, gives her a shy smile.

"Rob, I hear that you're also in the field of law." Mr. Wright turns to Rob.

"Yes, Sir. I moved here recently from Phoenix. When John left to start a practice with Sarah, it opened up an opportunity for me. Thanks to John's recommendation, I was able to secure a position. Despite the small town location, it's a pretty prestigious firm," Rob states proudly.

"Well, welcome to Rosedale. It *is* a small town, but it's a friendly one and I think that you'll feel right at home here," Mr. Wright declares.

A BELL FOR CHRISTMAS

"Oh, I already am," Rob responds, as he gives Jessica a big smile.

Sarah feels a hand on her shoulder. She turns around to see Judge Joe Conner standing behind her.

"Judge Joe! Come in, come in. Join our little circle of warmth!" Sarah grabs his arm and pulls him in.

"Liz! Jim! Good to see you!" Judge Joe gives hugs all around. "Rob, welcome! It's nice to see you outside of the courtroom for a change."

Rob gives Judge Joe a strong handshake. "Thanks Judge. Same here."

"My guess is that Santa is getting ready for the big lighting ceremony?" Judge Joe looks at the huge tree towering nearby.

"Yep. Santa and Elf Baxter are preparing for the onslaught of kiddies." Sarah grins.

"It's an honorable position! The Mayor chose well," Judge Joe states.

"It's John's third year as Santa, so it looks like the position may be permanent!" Sarah sips her hot chocolate. "He really does enjoy it and the children seem to love him too."

"It's a magical time for children. I played Santa many times myself. I think I got more from it than they did." Judge Joe shares, looking at the Christmas tree with fond memories.

"Judge Joe, may I speak to you for a moment about Bell?" Sarah asks, pulling him away from the group.

"Oh, Bell! Yes, the case you've been researching," the Judge nods his head.

"Well, it's not a case, but I have been looking into the situation. As you know, there's still a chance that Emma could be removed. John and I did some research and saw the Debutante announcement, as you mentioned. We saw that she was born at the Benton mansion and that the home is still under the Benton estate ownership. We have a lot more to investigate, but so far there seems to be a big gap from southern socialite to street person," Sarah shares.

"*If* she is a street person," the Judge adds.

"What do you mean?" Sarah asks.

"I don't really know, but if the home is in the Benton name and Bell is a Benton, then she may very well be living there." The Judge looks closely at Sarah and pauses. "It seems that you're more intrigued with Bell and *her* story than simply saving Emma. Is that true?"

Sarah looks at her feet and grins. "There may be some truth to that. The more I know, the more I don't know, and the more I want to know. I'm curious as to how someone like Bell could end up . . . end up,"

"Crazy? Lost? A misfit?" the Judge completes her thoughts.

"I don't know if I'd put it that way, but yes, I suppose that's what most people would think."

"And what do you think?" the Judge tilts his head, watching her.

"I don't know. My logic tells me that she's an emotionally unstable person. My heart tells me that there's something more to Bell that is worth exploring." Sarah looks up at the Judge, waiting for his response.

"Well, you know by now that we never lose when we listen to our heart. You've always let it guide you in the past," he smiles.

"Actually, not always. I've judged others and drawn false conclusions many times," she responds.

"And?" he asks.

"And I learned that it never serves me well. That's why I can't seem to shake off this mystery," she answers.

"Well, don't bother trying to find any mental health records for her," the Judge says looking up at the tree and watching the crowd. "You won't find much about Bell Benton there. Although with a little more research you would find that she was engaged at one time." The Judge continues to watch the crowd acting somewhat detached from the conversation.

"Engaged? But not married?" Sarah asks, her mouth open in astonishment.

"Yep. Engaged but never married. Spent her life alone, she did." The Judge pulls out a pipe and slowly lights it.

Sarah stands in silence, staring at him. She realizes that as she and John suspected, he possesses more knowledge on the subject. In usual 'Judge Joe' form, information was doled out in parcels, to be explored and mulled over. Nothing was ever handed over in a neat package. One was expected to earn information and make their own discoveries along the way. Sarah watches him as he takes his time, puffing on the pipe to get it fully ignited. He finally pulls in a mouthful of smoke and blows it out, then takes in a deep breath of fresh air.

"Yep, they never made it down the aisle. There was a tragic accident and he was lost before the marriage took place. Bell was heart broken, as you can imagine." Sarah moves in closer so as not to miss a word. He looks at Sarah with a sad expression. "Bell may act crazy, but I think she's just sad. I can tell you that she doesn't belong in a mental facility. She's of sound mind, that old gal. I do know that for sure. After the death of her fiancé, she spent the rest of her years in seclusion at the mansion taking care of her parents in their later years until their deaths. Never seemed to pull out of her sorrow." The Judge takes a small puff on his pipe. "Maybe that *is* crazy."

"That's heart wrenching!" Sarah responds.

"She has Emma now, a stray that she found. As you know, they've walked the streets of Rosedale for years. Who knows why and who knows what happens to a person when they've lost all hope." The Judge reaches out to Sarah and places his hand on her shoulder. "Sarah, whatever happened to Bell was *her* journey and she's made her own choices along the way. You shouldn't get too concerned about the past. We only have today and need to move forward the best that we can. I suggest that you find out if she still lives in the house and if so, determine what those conditions are. I'm sure that Emma has a warm bed at night, aren't you?"

"I guess." Sarah looks at the Judge still saddened at the story. "And

I know you're right. The past is the past and all we can do is to offer our help now."

"That's right. Focus on your goal." He pauses. "It's to make sure that Bell doesn't lose Emma, right?" He looks at Sarah who is silent. "Right, Sarah?"

Sarah nods her head. "It's just that, well, it's Christmas. You know?" The Judge raises his eyebrows. "Yeah, I'll look into the mansion."

"Good girl! Let me know what you find and if you feel that Emma is safe and secure, I'll put in a word with Animal Control. Deal?" He puts his hand out with his palm up.

Sarah slaps his hand. "Deal!"

The Judge turns to Mr. and Mrs. Wright. "Jim? Liz? Are you up for a hot mulled wine?"

"We'd love one!" Mrs. Wright answers. "Mrs. Costello? Would you like a mulled wine?"

Mrs. Costello turns to Mr. Wright. "Jim, since you're pushing me home, I'm officially not driving! Count me in!" she laughs.

"Great. I'll be back in a moment. Keep my spot!" the Judge orders and is quickly off to a vendor.

Sarah stares at him as he walks off. "She was engaged. Wow," she whispers to herself.

"What?" Jessica asks as she steps back to Sarah's side.

"Oh, nothing. I was just talking to myself," Sarah answers. "Rob, how is your house hunting going? Have you found a renovation project yet?"

"I have," Rob answers. "I'm in the middle of closing on a place. It's a cute home, over 100 years old and needs a lot of work. Just like I like 'em."

"We're going to work on it together," Jessica adds. "It's exciting and fun!"

"We'll see how much fun she thinks it is when she's all dirty and taking a sledge hammer to walls every weekend!" Rob adds.

"That sounds exciting!" Jessica claps her hands like a child.

"I don't think I've ever seen her this giddy about hard labor! Rob, you certainly have a way with Jessica," Sarah teases.

"I hope so." Rob pulls Jessica close to him and puts his arms around her. Jessica beams with happiness.

Mayor Roberts takes his place on a small stage placed in front of the large tree. The crowd gathers around in anticipation of the big event.

"Ladies and gentlemen, family and friends, I would like to thank you for coming to the Rosedale Annual Tree Lighting ceremony. As you know, I am Mayor Max Roberts and I would like to thank the Parson Family Farm which, once again, donated this incredible tree!" The audience applauds as the Parson Family steps forward and waves to the crowd. "And now, the moment we've been waiting for, the switch that will kick off our holiday season here in Rosedale for all to enjoy. May we all count down? Ten!"

"Nine! Eight! Seven! Six! Five! Four! Three! Two! One! Yaaaaaaaaaay!" The crowd claps and cheers as Mayor Roberts flips the switch that illuminates the towering evergreen. It dazzles and sparkles, bringing light to the entire square.

"Whoopee!" Mrs. Costello yells, clapping. "I never get tired of this!"

"Neither do I," Mrs. Wright agrees.

"And now, I'd like to announce that Santa has come all the way from the North Pole to visit Rosedale! Children, line up and put in your orders! I would like to thank the Merry Minstrel Singers who will entertain us this evening. Happy Holidays to all of you! I am now going to hand the stage over to our talented entertainment," the Mayor announces.

A group of men and women join him on the stage and set up their microphones. They begin to sing holiday songs in harmony to the delight of the crowd.

"I guess that means that your husband will get to work now!" Mr. Wright says as Sarah watches the stage.

"Yes, he's going to be a busy man." Sarah looks to see John and Baxter seated at the side of the tree. A helper organizes the children who form a long line.

Judge Joe appears with a large tray of hot mulled wine.

"God bless you, Joe!" Mrs. Costello cheers as she pulls the first cup from the tray.

"Everyone? Please, join me in a holiday toast." Judge Joe passes the cups out to the group. "To a bright holiday season and new beginnings!"

"Cheers! To new beginnings!" The friends raise their glasses and toast.

Judge Joe looks at Sarah and smiles. She shakes her head at him and grins.

Chapter Six
Nothing Like Popovers

"That man is so frustrating!" Sarah picks up a vase and examines it.

"What man?" John sorts through the display of cookware on a shelf in front of him and looks around the store at the overwhelming gift options.

"Judge Joe, that's who!" Sarah extends her arm, showing John the vase.

"It's pretty, but your Mom will be much happier with something she can use, like this cookware." John picks up a set of knives. "Or these cutting knives. These are really good ones. I think she'd appreciate something like this." John looks at Sarah who is noticeably distracted.

"Sarah, focus. What's bothering you so much? So Judge Joe told you Bell had been engaged. You wait until now to let this bother you? What's the big deal?" He continues to walk down the aisle, examining the extensive kitchen utensil inventory.

"What's the big deal? He could have told us that the first time. It's like he's holding back information. He does that, you know. Remember the last time he did this? Made us research right up until Christmas? It's like a puzzle that he wants other people to solve for some strange reason. We're all supposed to figure everything out for ourselves." Sarah flips through a stack of pot holders and kitchen towels, not truly paying attention to them.

"Yeah, and look at what happened. It forced us to actually get to know each other and we ended up married!" John turns to face Sarah. "Hon, I hate to side with Judge Joe, but there was no reason to know that Bell was engaged. How does that help with the issue of Emma? Sarah, you're treating this like a court case of yours. You're supposed to find out whether or not Emma has a safe, warm place to live. I'm sure Judge Joe didn't even think that it was relevant, and frankly it isn't. Why the obsession with all of this?"

"I just think we should have all of the facts, that's all." Sarah follows John through the aisles as he examines more gift options.

"I think the closer we get to Christmas, the more Bell and Emma out there on their own is bothering you. She just became a real person." John watches as Sarah continues to stare into space. "Are you going to help me? This is your Mom, after all. You would know better than I would, what she'd want." He looks at Sarah and sees that she is totally preoccupied. "Hello! Sarah Wright, come back to me!" John snaps his fingers.

"Yeah, O.K." Sarah pauses.

"I have an idea. Let's go have lunch and talk about it so that you can get it off of your mind. Then we'll get back to gift shopping, O.K.?" John takes Sarah's chin and raises it to look her in the eyes.

"Lunch sounds good." She puts her arm around him. "I'm sorry. But, you know me. When I get into something,"

"You're in it all the way. Yeah, I *do* know you! That's why we're going to go take a break and get it all out there so that you can concentrate and enjoy our day." John takes her hand and walks her out of the home goods area of the department store and to an escalator. They ride up another floor and exit, heading toward the corner to the store restaurant. A hostess greets them.

"It'll be about 10 minutes before I can seat y'all. Perhaps you'd like to sit at the counter and wait?" she asks.

"No, we're fine here," John answers. They step aside and sit on a bench at the entrance. Sarah is silent. "Hey, isn't that your Mom and Dad?" John asks.

"What? Where?" Sarah looks up.

"Over there in the corner at a table." John looks toward them and waves. A couple waves back. "Yep, it is. Come on, they're at a four top. Let's see if they want company."

John and Sarah greet her parents who are pleased to see them. A large bag sits at the base of the table.

"Well this is a surprise! Hello you two love birds!" Mrs. Wright looks down at her bag. "No peeking! We were Christmas shopping. That and your Dad loves the popovers they serve before each meal."

"They're free! And they're *huge*, with a crispy top and a hollow interior. Except the bottom piece. That's all soft and melts in your mouth. I think it's some kind of French muffin or something fancy like that," Mr. Wright says with excitement.

"Jim, they're popovers not muffins. That's why they call them popovers." Mrs. Wright shakes her head and looks at Sarah and John. "See? He loves them." Mrs. Wright grins.

"Oh, I know about Dad and the popovers. I can't say I don't love them myself," Sarah adds. "Do you mind if we join you?"

"Don't be silly. Sit down! Its wonderful to see you. I take it you were doing some Christmas shopping yourself?" Mrs. Wright asks.

"We were, but Sarah has been a bit preoccupied, so we thought we'd eat lunch before tackling our list." John adds.

"Sarah? What are you so preoccupied with? I hope it's not work," Mr. Wright states.

"No Dad, it's not work. It's something else that I'm concerned with," she answers.

"It must be something pretty important," Mrs. Wright says.

"Let me just say that it involves the welfare of an animal, if that gives you a hint," John raises an eyebrow and looks at Sarah.

"Oh my gosh! Not an animal case! You'll never get her attention now. What is it? Another rescue? Watch out, John, she'll have the house filled with them!" Mr. Wright teases.

"Oh Dad, it's not a rescue. Well, not exactly." Sarah frowns.

John interjects. "It's old lady Bell and her dog Emma."

"Animal Control got a complaint about Emma and she could lose the dog. I'm just trying to help out. You know, just make sure the situation doesn't get serious," Sarah explains.

"Why is that bothering you so much?" Mrs. Wright asks. "Why on earth would you be thinking of that while you're out shopping?"

"It's Bell and her past that's so interesting," John says, as he picks up a menu.

"Did I miss something here? Bell, old lady Bell is interesting?" Mr. Wright asks. A waitress approaches the table and sets down a plate of popovers. "Oh, and could you bring another plate of these? Our daughter and son-in-law will be joining us." The waitress nods and leaves.

"Oh please! Who are you kidding? You wanted more for yourself!" Mrs. Wright says.

"I do not!" Mr. Wright grabs a popover and stuffs a pad of butter inside it, smiles and takes a bite. "Ahhhh. Heaven!" He pauses and looks at Sarah and John with a big smile.

"Oh, honey! Don't worry. She's been fine all of these years. I'm sure you'll be able to help her!" Mrs. Wright claims her own popover.

"Did you know Bell was engaged at one time?" John asks.

"Bell? Old lady Bell was engaged?" Mr. Wright's eyes widen.

"Oh Jim, stop calling her that!" Mrs. Wright frowns.

"Yeah. Who would have guessed. Of course, that was when she was much younger. Judge Joe told Sarah," John shares.

"He did and he waited to share that information like it was a secret or something," she says with a look of disapproval.

"Well, maybe he didn't think it was necessary for you to know," Mr. Wright adds.

"That's what I said," John agrees.

"That old woman was once young too and I'm sure she had a life like anyone else. Besides, we don't always have to know everything about people's private lives," Mr. Wright says taking another bite.

"Like Judge Joe? He's never been married. Considering that I grew up around him, I find it odd that I don't know anything about his personal life except that he comes from a wealthy family, much like the Bentons. He seemed to know the family and their social circles." Sarah says.

"Well, he never married, but he was engaged too," Mrs. Wright reveals without so much as a look at the others.

"Mom!" Sarah exclaims.

"What?" Mrs. Wright looks up and sees Mr. Wright give her a look of disapproval. "Jim, is that a secret?"

"Liz, I don't know if it's a secret, but you know Joe. He likes to maintain mystery." Mr. Wright looks at Sarah in anticipation of questions.

"Oh, you know I've got to hear about this!" Sarah is noticeably excited. "Judge Joe was engaged?"

"Yes he was. As you know, Joe and I attended law school together. Well during that time, when your Mom and I were dating, Joe was dating someone too. Actually, the love of his life. A gal he met here in Rosedale. They dated throughout their teen years. He was a few years older and went off to college while she remained in Rosedale. She ended up moving and that was that."

"What do you mean that was that? She just moved and they never spoke again?" Sarah asks.

"Something like that. Joe was in another city at school and the gal's father wanted her to get an education, also. She was really talented. An artist. She ended up going away to a prestigious art school and the relationship ended. He had asked her to marry him and was going to tie the knot when he graduated. Well, it never happened."

"Did you ever get to meet her?" Sarah asks, perking up.

"Oh sure. Your Mom and I met her many times. We'd all spend time together, go on double dates. A nice girl. Gabby was her name. Yes, very pretty and adored Joe." Mr. Wright looks at Mrs. Wright. "I don't think he ever got over that, do you?" Mrs. Wright shakes her head in agreement. "He never found anyone after that. Remained a wealthy bachelor, graduated from law school, eventually became a Judge. I can't help but think that he didn't want to leave here in hopes that she would one day return."

"Why don't you know more about her?" Sarah asks.

"Sarah, remember, your Dad and I didn't meet Joe until law school. He had already been to Harvard and had a life here in Rosedale that we were not a part of." Mrs. Wright reminds her.

"Oh my gosh, this is shocking!" Sarah exclaims. "Why didn't you ever share this?"

"What for? You never asked and it never was a topic of conversation," Mr. Wright says.

"See? This is a typical guy thing. They just don't think these things are important. I think it's very important! It's so romantic and tragic at the same time. Judge Joe, in love!" Sarah's face expresses deep concern.

"And this is exactly why us men *don't* share these things because you women make a big deal out of it." Mr. Wrights states, winking at John.

"But he's like an Uncle to me, Dad," Sarah reminds him.

"And he is a prominent figure in the community and a Judge. *Your* Judge, that you work with on a regular basis! There are things best kept private, Sarah. Not everyone is an open book like you!" Mr. Wright states.

"Oh, she's not totally an open book," John says. "Sarah keeps a lot to herself, too! Remember, Sarah? When we first reunited? You kept a lot of things to yourself," John cocks his head to one side and looks at her through one eye.

"We're not talking about me right now." She quickly picks up the menu and starts reading it.

"Yep, I didn't think so," John smiles and winks back at Mr. Wright.

Sarah shakes her head. "That is so romantic! Judge Joe engaged!

So sweet. It breaks my heart. The love of his life!" She thinks for a moment. "So, why didn't he," she begins.

"Ah! Don't go there. I can't answer that. I don't know why he didn't hunt her down or if he did. I don't know what happened to her or if they stayed in touch. He's a private man when it comes to those things. You'd have to ask him yourself," Mr. Wright peers up from his popover and gives her a stare. "Good luck with that." He smiles.

"Yeah, don't I know!" Sarah pauses and grins. "I just think it's so cool! Judge Joe in love! What a surprise."

"Your Dad and I really liked her. But, she was young. We all were young. You make the best decisions you can at the time, with what you know. Things happen and life goes on!" Mrs. Wright comments.

"Oh my gosh!" Sarah gasps.

John watches her. "What?"

"Well, Judge Joe told me that Bell lost her fiancé to an accident. I can't help but think that he somehow empathizes with her."

"No doubt," Mr. Wright says. "He can be mysterious, Joe can. Doesn't share a whole lot. I agree, Sarah. It sounds like Bell and Joe have that in common."

The waitress reappears with two extra plates of popovers bringing a big smile to Mr. Wright's face. "May I take your orders?" she asks.

Mr. Wright orders for himself and Mrs. Wright. John and Sarah do the same.

"That Rob sure is a nice young man, isn't he?" Mrs. Wright asks, directing her question to Sarah.

"He really is. I don't think I've ever seen Jessica this excited about someone. I think this could be the real deal!" Sarah shares.

"Well, we're so happy for her. She's waited a long time for the right person." Mrs. Wright places a popover on Sarah's plate and begins to cut it up. "So, Rob mentioned that he renovates old homes?"

"Yeah, he's really into it," John says. "I've seen a couple of his home flips and they're beautiful. There are a few he has his eye on here in Rosedale. He's really skilled at it and I would bet that he'd rather renovate homes than practice law."

"Oh really? Well, that would be nice. Jessica seemed pretty excited about getting involved with that," Mr. Wright comments. "Those two could be a nice team."

"That's what we think," Sarah says. "It was John's idea to introduce them. Rob's an old friend of his. We're excited to have such a fun couple to hang out with," Sarah sips her water as the waitress shows up with appetizers, placing them in the center of the table.

"That's so nice! Who knows what the future holds for them! Look at you two! Coming up on your very first wedding anniversary!" Mrs. Wright smiles, her mouth full.

John reaches over and holds Sarah's hand. "The first of many," he adds.

"I hope you get to be a happy old married couple like your Mom and me," Mr. Wright says as he leans over and kisses Mrs. Wright.

"Yep, I still love your Dad as much as ever," Mrs. Wright places her hand on his. "Now, come on and let's eat so that we can get back to our shopping."

Sarah is deep in thought. John watches her. "Oh no. I see those wheels turning. I'm afraid this conversation about the Judge has made things worse. Now you'll never be able to focus today."

"No, I'm good, actually. Somehow I feel better. My heart goes out to Judge Joe. Things are making more sense. Maybe he's been grieving too. Not like Bell, but in his own way. It explains a lot of things about him." Sarah pauses. "Come on, let's eat and get our shopping done." Sarah smiles at John and kisses him.

"That's a good start!" He smiles. The waitress brings their main meals and they enjoy their afternoon together before parting ways with the Wrights.

Chapter Seven
Gus Makes a Great Shepherd's Pie

"Knock! Knock!" Sarah yells as she opens the front door of the wood and brick bungalow. The door squeaks as she pushes it open, peeking her head in.

"Sarah? Is that you? Come on in!" Rob shouts from a back room.

Jessica soon appears from a hallway. The empty interior echoes her footsteps. "It's not much to look at now, but it's got good bones. Come on in out of the cold and we'll show you around."

Sarah views the living room with its peeling plaster walls, high ceilings and heavy crown molding. The wide wood plank floors are worn and dull, but solid. "It looks pretty good to me! Cute exterior too."

"Yeah, cute, but it needs a good scrub and paint job. Fortunately, most of the interior is cosmetic except the kitchen. That's a total gut job!" Jessica says.

Rob appears and joins them. "Welcome to my latest project! What do you think?"

"I was just telling Jessica that it looks like a gem to me. What are the plans?" Sarah asks.

"Come see the kitchen." Rob leads the way to the back of the house. "I'm actually going to move in and slowly renovate. Like Jessica said, it's mostly cosmetic with updates to the bathrooms and the kitchen overhaul. Otherwise, no major projects unless I run into a surprise or two. You never know what you'll run into with these old homes. My goal is to get this place looking as pretty as it was 100 years ago."

"With some modern touches, of course!" Jessica adds.

The three head to the kitchen with its original tiles and cupboards intact. "This is beautiful. I can see the possibilities!" Sarah says.

"Pretty, but not practical. I'll replace all of the cupboards. This will be a real test for Jessica," Rob looks at Jessica with a grin. "She'll get an introduction to what a *real* renovation entails."

"I'm ready! Put me to work!" Jessica laughs.

"Oh right. You're laughing now!" Rob pats her on the back.

"Well, I think it'll be fun," Sarah comments. "But, don't count on me to be swinging a sledge hammer with Jessica. I can, however, be bribed with pizza to paint a wall or two!"

"You may be sorry you offered!" Jessica teases.

"Never!" Sarah says. "It'd be my pleasure. Rob, you're bringing good things to Rosedale."

"I hope so," he grins.

"Hey, Sarah, I'll go get the plans," Jessica says. "They're out in the car. I'll be right back." She leaves the two, puts on her coat and walks out the front door.

Rob turns to Sarah. "I'm really thankful, Sarah."

"For?" Sarah asks.

"The introduction. Jessica's a great gal. We're having a lot of fun and, well, I'm thinking that there could be a future together." He tilts his head as he looks at Sarah and smiles.

"Oh really? That sounds pretty serious!" Sarah is surprised at the admission.

"I wanted to ask you about something. You've been talking about the Benton mansion lately." He waits for Sarah's response.

"Yeah. We aren't sure, but Bell may live there. You know the elderly woman with the dog," she says.

"Right. I know. You and John mentioned that. So, I take it that she owns the place?" he asks.

"It's in the family name, but whether or not Bell has any ownership, we can't be sure. Why do you ask?" Sarah asks.

"I've been looking around town for homes to renovate, as you know. I've been out to the Benton mansion several times. It would be a dream of mine to take on something so grand and historic. It's a big project, but exactly what I've been looking for. Of course, if things work out with Jessica and me," he says with a smile.

"Ohhhhh, I see! Then you would move into the house? Now that would be awesome. But, I have to ask you. You said you've been out to the mansion. Did you by any chance notice any activity? Anyone inside, or footsteps around the place?"

"No. Nothing. I think it's abandoned. My guess is that it's been deserted for quite some time. I would hate to see that place eventually go to the bull dozers. If it isn't taken care of soon, I'm afraid that's what will happen."

"John and I were going to go out to the Benton place," Sarah shares. "Are you absolutely sure that no one could be living there, maybe going in a back way or something like that?"

"I've been out there quite a few times. I didn't realize it was the place you were referring to. It's in a remote area, but I looked around the property more than once. I was just out there a couple of days ago. It's a big piece of property, backed up to some dense woods. There are never any footprints nor paths, and the snow has collected up against all of the doors. It truly is deserted. Believe me, I would love to talk to the owner and find out if I could get a look and make an offer."

"You just saved us a trip." Sarah pauses as she hears the front door open. "And Rob, I'll keep your future plans between us." She smiles.

"Thanks. I'd appreciate that." He returns the smile. "Jessica! We're still in the kitchen!"

"What are you two chatting about?" Jessica asks as she enters with a set of blueprints.

"I was just telling Rob that John and I were going to head out to the Benton mansion. We wanted to find out if Bell is living there and Rob informed me that it's deserted," Sarah says.

"Oh, the Benton mansion. Yes, Rob is taken by that place," Jessica smiles at him.

"That's true. I drive by there whenever I can. I am sure that there's no way anyone lives there." Rob takes the blueprints and places them on the kitchen counter, slowly unrolling the layers of paper.

"What's up, Sarah?" Jessica asks, assisting Rob with the prints.

"Just trying to help Bell to keep her dog." Sarah looks at Jessica and thinks. "We can't seem to figure out where she and the dog live, if anywhere."

"Well, she doesn't bother anyone. Doesn't beg for money or anything like that. She doesn't act like she's poor other than looking pretty ragged. She's just a bit of an odd soul. Where could she possibly be going?" Jessica smooths out the blueprints and looks at the top page. "Sarah, this is what Rob's going to do with the kitchen. See this wall? It's coming out so that the kitchen and dining area will be open."

Sarah walks to the print and takes a look. "That's going to look incredible, Rob." She studies the new plan and pauses. "Rob, isn't there a basement door, or some other place she could get into that isn't obvious?"

"No, Sarah. I've walked the entire place. I even went back to the stables. No one's been there for many years." He looks at her with a sympathetic expression. "I really wish I could tell you different, but I'm *very* sure about this." Rob places his hand on her shoulder. "Sarah, it's a big house. It's not a place for an older lady to live. It would be cold and impossible to maintain."

"Yeah. I know. I was just hoping." Sarah looks at Rob and Jessica. "I'm sorry! I'm so preoccupied with all of this. Hey, let's take a look at these prints."

Jessica smiles and pulls the top print off, revealing the next page. "Here's the plan for the upstairs."

"What a transformation! This is going to be beautiful when you get done!" Sarah examines the plans, still deep in thought.

"Sarah?" Jessica grabs her hand.

"Yes?" Sarah looks at her with surprise.

"I just asked you a question. Are you O.K.?" Jessica watches Sarah's face.

Sarah shakes her head to clear out the thoughts. "I'm so sorry. What did you ask?" Sarah looks down at her feet, smiles and looks back at Jessica.

"That Bell mystery is really bothering you," Jessica states.

"Yeah, that and something I learned about Judge Joe," Sarah shares.

"Oh? What's that?" Jessica asks.

"Just that he was once engaged. He was deeply in love and they drifted apart and never got married. He never found anyone that he loved as much as he loved Gabby," Sarah says.

"I can't imagine that! He's always been such a tough guy. I never would have guessed that Judge Joe would be such a romantic," Jessica responds. "Is that her name? Gabby?"

"Yes. She moved away and that was the end." Sarah thinks for a moment. "Kind of makes sense in a lot of ways . . . you know, how he is so mysterious when it comes to his personal life. He's always there for everyone else, but we never know much about the Judge." Sarah looks at Jessica and Rob, "Hey, I'm truly sorry for being so unfocused."

"No, don't apologize. He's like family and I know it's personal. You care about Judge Joe. I totally get it," Jessica smiles.

"As for Bell, well, I just feel like no one should be alone at Christmas. She lost everything dear to her and I am determined that she won't lose her little Emma. It's just not right. I can't help but think that there's something more that I can do," Sarah adds.

Jessica puts her arm around Sarah. "Well, you're doing all that you can, Sarah. You're really good at solving problems, but we all have our limits as to just how much we can help someone. You can't bring back those people for Bell or Judge Joe."

"No, but I see Bell now, for the first time. So many years, Bell has passed by and I looked right through her. We all have. It's never too late to change that," Sarah says.

"You're right about that, Sarah. But, what can you do? What can any of us do?" Jessica asks.

"Well, I thought I was finally on to something, but now that Rob told me that no one could possibly be in the mansion, I'm stumped. If I can at least make sure that Emma is safe and let Bell know that she has people that support her, then I'll feel that I've accomplished something." Sarah looks at Rob who nods in agreement.

"You're going to have to follow her, Sarah. It's intrusive, but if that's what it takes to find out, then you don't have much of a choice," Jessica suggests.

"I think you're right." Sarah looks at Rob and Jessica. "Have either of you seen her lately?"

"I haven't seen her in a couple of weeks," Jessica answers. Rob shakes his head.

"I'm sorry to say that the last time I saw her, I scared her off." Sarah pauses. "Do me a favor. If either of you see Bell, can you please let me know immediately. I *am* going to get to the bottom of this. I'm not sure exactly what I can do to change her circumstances, but I have the feeling that I'll know when I get there." She turns and starts to leave. "Rob, Jessica, this place is going to be beautiful! I can't wait to see the finished product. Please excuse me, but I need to get to the courthouse and drop off some papers."

Rob and Jessica walk her to the door.

"Will you be joining us on Christmas Eve, Rob? My parents have a small gathering every year as Jessica knows. We'd love for you to be a part of our celebration. May we count on you?" Sarah asks.

"You sure can. Thanks for the invite," Rob answers.

"Now go! Go solve your mystery! You know that we support whatever you do and you can count on us for anything," Jessica says, nudging her.

"Thanks," Sarah hugs her. "I appreciate that." She smiles.

Rob and Jessica walk Sarah to the porch, bid farewell and watch her get in her car and drive away.

"That's my Sarah!" Jessica smiles. She turns to Rob. "I do hope that she figures this out and if I know my girl like I think I do, she's not going to stop until she does!"

Rob watches as the snow begins to fall. "I have the feeling that you're right." He pulls Jessica close and puts his arm around her. They watch Sarah's car disappear at the end of the street.

❦

"If it isn't our Claire, looking all happy!" Sarah leans over the counter at the courthouse entrance. Behind it Claire sits on her rolling chair, filing papers in a cabinet behind her desk and humming a Christmas tune. She turns around.

"Well good day, Sarah! It *is* a glorious day, or almost evening actually!" she smiles, her rosy cheeks shining.

"Anything in particular that's putting that big smile on your face?" Sarah signs in.

"Yes ma'am! My daughter's flying in for Christmas. She lives in Boston now so we don't get to see her very often. She and her husband, along with my two grandkids are coming to stay for a week!"

"Claire, that's wonderful! I hope that we get to meet them!" Sarah hands Claire some paperwork.

"Oh, you can count on me showing those grandkids off! You'll see us around town!" She looks at the documents. "I see that you don't have any cases today. Just filing these, Sarah?"

"Yep. It should all be in order," Sarah watches as Claire flips through each page.

Claire places the papers in a wire basket on her desk. "They look good. I'll take care of it, Sarah. Now you have a nice evening!" Claire smiles and rolls around on her swivel chair, back to her filing cabinets and resumes her Christmas humming.

"Is that Sarah Rivera?" Sarah spins around to see Judge Joe approaching her from the hallway.

"Well, hello Judge Joe! Is it the end of your day?" she asks.

"Yes it is, and I'm off to one of my favorite spots, The Horseshoe Grill across the street," he announces.

"One of my favorites too!" Sarah says with little enthusiasm. "Well, have a wonderful meal."

The Judge walks up to her and stops. He looks her in the eyes and tilts his head. "Something bothering you, young lady?"

"Why no, why would you ask that?" Sarah looks at him with surprise.

"It's written all over your face." He pauses and smiles. "Sarah, are you available for a quick dinner at the grill? My treat."

Sarah contemplates the invitation. "John's going to be home soon and,"

"Oh John is probably still at the office, and I'm confident that he is capable of making his own dinner," the Judge interrupts.

Sarah laughs. "Actually, he does most of the cooking."

"See? Just as I thought. Come! Let's go visit like we used to." The Judge takes Sarah's arm and places it over his as he escorts her out of the courthouse.

"Bye Claire!" Sarah shouts.

Claire leans over and sticks her head out of the reception window as she watches the two leave. She smiles and nods to herself. "You have a good night Miss Sarah," she says quietly.

Judge Joe and Sarah make the short walk across the street to the quaint building that looks more like a log cabin than a restaurant. They enter the shower size foyer covered with pine and wood plank flooring where a hostess stand displays a sign "Seat Yourself."

"Shall we?" The Judge sweeps his hand away from Sarah, like an actor bowing, gesturing for her to enter. The two enter the small, but open room with log walls and worn carpets. It appears to be more like a private living room than a restaurant, with small areas where chairs and tables are placed.

"Hey Gus!" Judge Joe shouts at the burley man behind the grill in the open kitchen. In front of it is a bar where several patrons sit eating.

Gus waves, flames shooting up as he flips a burger. "Hey Joe! You son of a..."

"I have a young lady with me, Gus. Hold the vinegar!" Judge Joe laughs.

"Oh sorry, Joe! Welcome, young lady! Grab a seat and we'll take care of you. Margaret! Get these two a drink on the house!"

"Barbara and Leslie! How are you gals tonight?" Judge Joe asks, waving to the women behind the bar.

"We're well, Joe! We're well! Sit wherever you'd like!" Leslie shouts back.

At the center of the room is a fireplace with burning logs, now glowing a bright red. The Judge walks over to it and removes a log from a stack of wood sitting next to it. He places it on top of the burning pile, grabs a poker and pushes it onto the smoldering embers, igniting a spark and causing the log to catch fire. The light from the blaze fills the room with a golden glow.

"I do love a good fire on a chilly night! Why don't we take a seat here at my favorite spot?" Judge Joe gestures to the two sturdy, down filled chairs positioned in front of, and facing, the fireplace. A small table with a dim table lamp is positioned between them.

"This is my favorite spot too," Sarah says as she plops down in one of the chairs.

"Joe! The usual?" Margaret asks.

"Make it two!" Judge Joe shouts back. Margaret nods her head. He settles into his chair and turns to Sarah. "So, young lady. How is everything going?"

"Everything's great. John, the practice, Baxter, my parents, the house, it's all great," she answers.

"Then what's on your mind?" He watches her face.

"Nothing," Sarah stares into the fireplace.

"Oh, I've known you long enough to know when our Sarah isn't herself. If I was a betting man, I'd say there's something brewing in that pretty head of yours and I have a good idea what it is." He looks at Sarah with a serious face. "Go ahead, Sarah, and ask me whatever you'd like. Let's see if we can put your mind at ease."

Sarah continues to stare into the fireplace, contemplating what she will or will not say. She takes a deep breath and slowly releases it.

Margaret appears at the table with two short glasses, filled with bourbon. "Your private stash, Joe. Gus is picking up the tab. Shall I wait a while for your order?" she asks as she watches Sarah and smiles.

"Please do, and thank you Margaret." The Judge picks up Sarah's glass from the table and nudges her. "Here. This will warm you up."

Sarah looks up and accepts the drink. "Oh, thank you." Sarah sniffs the glass. "Bourbon?"

"Good guess," he smiles. "Now take a sip and let's have a chat."

Sarah sniffs the glass again and makes a grimace. She holds her breath and takes a small sip, coughs briefly and takes a breath of fresh air to clear her nostrils of the fumes.

"Well, I've been thinking that I've lived my entire life in Rosedale and I know so little." Sarah looks up at the Judge.

"Such as?" he asks.

"Bell for starters. Her family's been here for many years and I had no idea who she was." Sarah takes another small sip.

"Why do you feel you should have known? The Benton family hasn't been a part of the community for some time now. As for Bell, she has retreated from society altogether. Why should you be required to know everyone and their story?"

"I don't know. I feel a bit guilty about it. It just feels neglectful in some way." Sarah pauses and looks at the Judge. "Maybe selfish."

"Selfish? Oh Sarah, don't be silly. Let me tell you something. We didn't come here to solve everyone's problems. We came here to be the best we can be. Sometimes helping others too much interferes with their life lessons; the ones that are critical to their spiritual growth." He pauses. "It's true that we should support one another, be giving, loving, and compassionate. But don't confuse that with 'saving' someone who may not want to be saved or *needs* to experience struggle to appreciate joy. Bell, for instance," he pauses and takes a large sip of Bourbon. "Bell came from a good family, has money, had many choices available to her along the way like we all do. Your assumption is that Bell is dissatisfied with those choices, that she should be living a different kind of life."

"Well, shouldn't she? Judge Joe, I can't even figure out where she lives! And you see the way that she dresses," Sarah adds.

"She's not on the street begging, Sarah. As for her attire, well, again it's a choice. We assume because she isn't well dressed that something is somehow 'wrong.' But, she's warm. The dog is well cared for. Until we find a reason to intervene, then we need to be respectful of others life choices and paths. What may be crazy to some is perfectly acceptable to others."

Sarah takes a sip of Bourbon and thinks. "I never thought of it that way."

The Judge pats her shoulder. "That's because you're a loving and caring person. Nothing wrong with that, Sarah. But be careful to separate how you 'think' things should be and how they are supposed to play out for the good of that person and the good of all."

"I don't completely understand," Sarah looks at him.

"I mean that you want people to exist in a certain way because you think that 'certain way' is better, is right, and will make them happy. Sometimes the hardened journey is what brings them to appreciation, motivation, and even revelation. Don't rob them of that." He watches Sarah stare into the fire. "Your Bell, well there's a reason to intervene to some extent. We don't want to see Emma removed. No good would come of that, so we can take action. Beyond that, you need to be careful. With struggle comes great breakthroughs."

Sarah watches the Judge who now looks into the fire and leans back into his chair.

"Is that what happened to you?" Sarah asks.

Judge Joe looks at her, his face softens and he gives her a knowing look. "What are you referring to, Sarah?"

"Losing the love of your life? The path you chose?" She watches him as a smile slowly forms and he looks deep into the fire, pushing further back into his chair.

"Hmmm. Now that's a complicated answer for a complicated question." The Judge cups both hands around his bourbon glass, warming it up. "I don't believe in coincidences, do you?" He looks at Sarah who shakes her head in agreement. "I think that things happen exactly the way that they should. Granted, we have some say as to how that plays out. We have the gift of choice. But, who is to say what is good or bad. Who is to say for sure why Gabby and I were not to be." The Judge nods to himself as though having a conversation in his head. "I never stopped loving that gal, and I never gave up hope that she would somehow come back into my life."

Sarah is amazed at how much the Judge is revealing. She is silent and continues to watch him as he takes his time, carefully conveying his thoughts.

"But, Sarah, I've learned something that most people haven't. It's what brings pain to so many. I've learned to accept things as they are. Oh, don't get me wrong, I'm not saying that I *like* some of the circumstances, or the lessons that have come my way. But, acceptance, well, that makes life much more pleasant." He pauses, taking a sip of bourbon and swishing it around inside his mouth. "Timing and circumstances were to separate me from my Gabby. She was so young and had so much of life to explore. And so many other reasons seemed to get in the way." He takes another sip. "Acceptance. That's what keeps a man sane. Acceptance is faith. We don't always have to know why. We just have to trust that it serves a good purpose and live with it."

Sarah, sinks deep into her chair, crosses her legs and takes a sip of Bourbon. She joins the Judge as they gaze into the fire. They both stare, silently for several minutes.

"But you could have tried to find her. Get her back. Couldn't you?" Sarah looks at him.

"Yes. I certainly could have. Gabby always knew I was here, whenever she needed or wanted me. But I knew that her art was important. Her Father saw promise in her and he supported her studies." He pauses. "I respect that. I wouldn't have robbed her of that." They sit in silence for a few more minutes. "Then time goes by, and well, my Gabby is a pretty gal. And a smart one at that." He looks at Sarah. "You would have liked her, Sarah. She had a great sense of humor, and she loved to laugh." He smiles.

"What happened to her?" Sarah asks.

"She eventually got married. She graduated, opened an art gallery, and had children. I'm pleased for her. She deserves to be happy," he looks at Sarah with a sad smile.

"You're a strong person." Sarah grins. "You *do* truly love her to let her go like that. That isn't an easy task."

"No it's not." The Judge takes a big sip of Bourbon. "Margaret! Another when you get the chance!" He pushes back into his chair. "She wouldn't have been happy here. Not back then. She needed to soar. She studied in Paris for a while, spent years living abroad and showed her art in exhibits across the U.S. I never would have robbed her of that." He pauses. "Still the same, I miss the gal. I sure do miss her." He turns and looks at Sarah. "Even after all of these years."

"I'm sorry," Sarah reaches out and touches his arm.

"Don't be sorry, my dear girl. Like I said, things happen and we don't know why, but we just have to trust it all. I'm fortunate to have loved so deeply."

"I guess that you can understand Bell's circumstances," Sarah adds.

"In a way, yes. I can't imagine a loss so final. It's a shame that she chose to retreat from the world." The Judge places his empty glass on the table and Margaret returns with a fresh one. "Thank you, darlin'," he says and takes a sip from the new drink. "So, Sarah, did you find out where Bell lives?"

"No, we didn't. I tried to speak with her, but that was a mistake. I just frightened her and now she'll never let me approach her. Then I was at Rob's new place and he informed me that he's been out to the Benton mansion several times. It's completely deserted without a sign of entry. He's sure that no one could possibly have entered the place. No tracks, snow drifts high against the doors, and not even a hint that anyone's been out to the stables."

"Interesting," the Judge replies. "I don't suppose anyone's tried to follow her?"

"That's been impossible. Like I shared, I scared her off and she just seems to have disappeared. I'll be lucky to gain her trust again. I told Rob and Jessica to let me know if they see her. That's all I can do for now. No one else seems to know a thing about her."

"Well, don't give up. I know you'll get to the bottom of this." The Judge pats Sarah's hand. "Shall we order?" He looks at her and they smile. "They have a great Shepherd's pie here."

Sarah nods. "That sounds good."

The Judge signals to Margaret. "Hey Gus! Two Shepherd's pies!"

"Coming up Joe!" Gus waves and nods his head.

"Now let's catch up on things like we used to do when you were in law school." The Judge looks at Sarah with a smile.

She looks back at him and clinks her glass against his. "Yeah. Let's catch up. I'd like that."

Chapter Eight
Queen Costello

"Mrs. Miller, where would I find death and marriage records?" Sarah sits in the library scouring through stacks of books.

"You're in the right pile, Sarah." Mrs. Miller walks to the long table scattered with papers and records, and pulls two large books out. "Start with these two." She looks at Sarah and smiles. "I'm so sorry that we don't have these computerized, Sarah. As I shared with you before, it's not on the top priority list for us and we only have two people who are capable of converting files."

"Mrs. Miller, you don't have to apologize. I completely understand. I just wish I knew what I was looking for."

"Well, all of the Benton family records should be right in these two books, unless you want to explore announcements and articles in the newspapers. Those would be on film, as you know," she shares.

"Thanks, Mrs. Miller." Sarah continues to go through the books sitting in front of her. There it was. Mr. and Mrs. Benton's death records. Both deceased by natural causes, in the home. Nothing unusual. No marriage records or any other activity for the Benton family. It was as though a switch was flipped and all activity at the once brilliant Benton home ceased.

"Hey sunshine." Sarah looks up to see John standing in front of her. "Now how did I know I'd find you here. You know, since it's a little slow at the office, I thought we'd have more free time together. But, here she is at the library and I don't need to guess what you're researching."

"I found Mr. and Mrs. Benton's death notices, but nothing else of interest."

"Is that so?" John takes a seat across from Sarah and places his face in his hands as he plants his elbows on the table.

"John, when was the last time that you saw Bell?" Sarah asks.

"Hmmm. It's been a while. Before you scared her off, actually," he grins.

"Don't remind me! That was a huge mistake," Sarah shakes her head.

"I'm sure that she's hiding out in some warm place." John looks at Sarah who is noticeably concerned. "I know that look," he says. "You want to go find her, don't you?"

"I do. I don't want to scare her off, but at this point I'm stumped. If we could just follow her," Sarah watches John as he purses his lips. "Do you have any ideas?"

John sighs. "Sarah, I really don't know what to do either." John looks off into the distance for a moment. "Sarah, it's just that," he pauses and sighs again.

"What? Is it something bad?" Sarah looks at him intently.

"No, it's not bad, it's just that, well . . . there are two of us now. It's not Sarah Wright, attorney at law, saving the world anymore. You have a partner who cares about you, supports you, and well," he pauses. "I love you Sarah. We're a team. You've been so entrenched in all of this that you can't even focus on anything else."

Sarah stares at him for a moment. "John, I'm so sorry. I know we're a team. I don't mean to shut you out." She watches him as he is deep in thought.

John leans across the table and takes her hand in his. "I know you don't mean to. But, things are different now. You've got to let me in, Sarah. Between Bell, Emma and the Judge, I feel like I've lost you. You even dream about it."

Sarah puts her hand over his. "I know. I've been a little crazy, huh?"

"No, not crazy. Obsessed maybe, but not crazy. Sarah, I'd do anything for you. You know that. We'll solve this case, but we're going to do it together. No more sneaking off to the library on your own, no more 'Nancy Drew takes on the world,' O.K.?"

"Sometimes I forget; you know?" Sarah frowns.

"Sarah, Bell lost her love and there's nothing that will bring him back, Judge Joe lost his love and who knows if that could have played out differently, but it's possible to lose someone even if you live under the same roof. Let's not let that happen. It's our first year of marriage. We've taken on a lot. Our own firm, working together, living together!" He kisses her hand. "All I know is that I love you, and I love having this incredible person next to me, every step of the way." John looks deep into her eyes. "No matter what, for better or worse, until the end, Sarah."

Sarah's eyes well up with tears. Her voice cracks. "I remember those vows. John," she kisses his hand. "I couldn't have asked for more. Can you forgive me?"

John gives her a big smile. "Oh, I can think of a few ways that you can make it up to me."

Sarah smacks his hand. "Oh you!"

John laughs and gets serious again. "Sarah, I want you to know that we're not just a team. We're one now. Do you get that?"

Sarah looks at him and gives him a sheepish grin. "Yeah. I do get that."

John leans back in his chair. "By the way, you had your phone shut off. I walked over here to remind you that we have a party to attend. Your parents' neighborhood holiday party? Remember?"

"Oh geez! Right! Sorry about that." Sarah looks down and shakes her head. "I just keep having to apologize, don't I? I was adhering to the no cell phone policy and got so engrossed in the records that I didn't check." Sarah pulls her cell phone out of her purse and looks at it. "Yep, here it is. 'Party in one hour,' text from John!"

John laughs. "You're forgiven, and you look beautiful. That was an hour ago. Let's walk over there now, O.K.?"

"Sure. Let me put these records away." Sarah stands and picks up several books and turns to John. "I love you."

John smiles and kisses her. "We can stop at the bakery on the way, and pick up a dessert." He picks up the remaining books and places them on a cart. "Bundle up. The snow's coming down pretty strong. That storm that was predicted is in full force."

"I'm prepared!" Sarah points to her boots. The two collect their belongings. John grabs Sarah's hand and she pulls close to him and puts her head on his shoulder.

"I'm a lucky girl," she says. "Now, let's get out of here."

<hr />

"Hello dear!" Mrs. Costello grabs Sarah's hand and gives it a squeeze.

"Mrs. Costello! So good to see you again," Sarah gives her a hug.

"Get over here, you handsome man!" Mrs. Costello reaches out to grab John's hand as he enters the Landis home. "Come give an old lady a hug!"

John squeezes into the crowded entry of the Landis living room and reaches down to hug Mrs. Costello who is snug in her wheelchair. "Mrs. Costello! You're looking very pretty tonight!"

"Oh, thank you John! Sarah, your Mother was nice enough to take me to the hairdresser this morning." She turns her head to show off her fresh perm.

"It's lovely," Sarah comments. "Is that a hint of purple I see?"

"Oh you noticed! It's the latest hair color. Lovely Lavender they call it." Mrs. Costello takes the palm of her hand and plumps up her curls.

"Well, it *is* lovely," John says, trying to hide a smile. "And very stylish!"

Sarah smiles at John and grabs his hand. "Mrs. Costello, can we get you something? We're going to make our way through this crowd to find Mr. Landis."

"A little something sweet would be nice. Oh and dear, could you freshen up my punch? I think that you'll find Mr. Landis in the dining room visiting with your parents. And your Mother brought a lovely cake," she says.

"Well, I'll be sure to get you a piece of that cake!" Sarah takes Mrs. Costello's cup and looks at it. "Punch?"

"Cranberry juice," Mrs. Costello winks at her. "With just a splash of vodka. It's a bit chilly and I need something to warm me up!" Sarah nods her head smiling. Mrs. Costello gives her an innocent smile.

"Yes. Of course, Mrs. Costello. We'll be right back." Sarah assures her as she and John turn to make their way through the crowded room of the guests all noisily chatting and laughing. "Mrs. Costello enjoys a little 'warm up' drink this time of year," Sarah says quietly to John.

"I see," he snickers. "Let's take care of that for her." They push through, greeting everyone. "I see your parents." John points to the back of the dining room where a table is filled with food and desserts. A drink table is set up against the back wall. John and Sarah finally squeeze their way through.

"There you are!" Mrs. Wright says. "Glad you made it!"

"Mom, Dad! Oh, and Mr. Landis," Sarah leans over to hug Mr. Landis who is speaking with the Wrights.

"Sarah and John, welcome to my home. I'm so pleased that you could make it!" he says, extending his hand.

"Mr. Landis, it's so good to be here. Thank you for hosting this wonderful party!" Sarah says, reaching to grab his hand.

"It's a full house!" Mr. Landis laughs. "It's good to have laughter in the place."

"It sure is," Sarah gives him a hug. "Mom, I hear you made a pretty nice cake. Mrs. Costello sent us on a mission to fetch her a piece! That and her cranberry juice."

"Hand me that cup, Sarah," Mr. Wright orders. "I'll fix Mrs. Costello's drink."

"Oh, Dad, you need to put . . ." Sarah begins.

"Yes, my dear girl, I know what goes into Mrs. Costello's holiday drink," Mr. Wright winks.

Sarah nods and laughs. "Mom, can you point out which cake is yours?" Sarah sees that the table is loaded with desserts.

"It's the one with the white icing and the little Christmas trees on the side, Sarah." Mrs. Wright points. "John, I'm really glad that you both made it."

"So am I. I had to hunt her down at the library. She snuck away to research our favorite subject," John reveals.

"Bell?" Mrs. Wright turns to Sarah. "So, what did you find out? I have to admit that I'm curious, myself."

"Not much else other than what I shared with you before." Sarah shrugs her shoulders.

"So, do you think she lives at the old mansion?" Mr. Wright asks.

"That's what John and I thought, but Rob has been out there several times to look at the place and he assures me that no one could possibly live there." Sarah answers. "Dad, can you hand me that cup? I'd better deliver Mrs. Costello her punch," Sarah turns and looks around the room when she sees Mrs. Costello rolling toward them.

"Excuse me, excuse me," she says, barreling through the crowd and running over a few toes along the way. She arrives at the dining room table where the four stand watching her approach. "I thought you forgot me!"

"I'm sorry Mrs. Costello. I started talking to my parents and got side tracked." Sarah leans down and hands her the glass cup, filled with her cranberry vodka concoction. "Just the way you like it. I'll cut you a piece of my Mom's cake," Sarah offers.

"This is fine for now. I'm running out of room here," Mrs. Costello holds the cup and sips from it. "So, what were you talking about that distracted you?" she asks.

"Oh, more discussion about Bell," Mr. Wright shares.

"Still? Sarah, what's so interesting about that old gal? Why I knew Bell years ago. We were friends when we were younger. She's really not that exciting. Just an old lady walking the streets with an overfed dog, mumbling to herself." Mrs. Costello takes a sip of her drink and pauses. "She's not crazy, you know."

"You knew her?" Sarah is amazed. Like Judge Joe, Mrs. Costello always seems to be a reluctant source of valuable information. "Why didn't you say something before?" Sarah asks, now totally engaged in the discussion.

"You didn't ask. Is it important? You were interested in the dog and where Bell goes at night. My childhood stories can't be of help there." Mrs. Costello looks totally relaxed.

"Mrs. Costello, what happened to her? How did she end up like that?" Sarah asks.

"She was engaged, you know. Had a nice, young beau. He loved his Bell, he did. And she, well she was smitten for sure. He was building their marital home. A beautiful little place." Mrs. Costello stops and sips her drink, pausing as though she was done with her story. She obviously enjoys the attention and savors it for a few more minutes.

Sarah is noticeably anxious. "What happened?"

"They never did wed. He built that lovely home, and the young man was killed in an accident. Fell from the roof. Tragic, it was. It devastated Bell. She mourned for years. Never dated, never went out of the house much after that. We never really saw Bell. She gave up on life."

"And that's it?" Sarah grabs a small plate and places a piece of her Mother's cake on it. She hands it to Mrs. Costello along with a fork and napkin. "Here, I'll hold your drink while you eat some cake."

"Oh, Sarah, how nice of you. You know how much I love this cake!" Mrs. Costello hands Sarah her glass while Mr. and Mrs. Wright snicker at the performance.

"So, you were saying that Bell never left the house after that?"

Sarah patiently waits as she watches Mrs. Costello slowly take a bite of cake, smacking the frosting.

"Oh, yes, I do love this cake." She pauses and wipes chocolate off of her lips. "So, as I was saying, Bell went into a sort of seclusion I guess you could call it. Turned into an old maid and then took care of her elderly parents until they died of old age." She takes another bite and smacks her lips. "My drink, dear?"

"Oh, of course." Sarah takes the plate of cake and hands Mrs. Costello her drink. She takes a sip and continues.

"So, there she was, a middle aged woman in that big house. No one to take care of it for her. She just let it decay and eventually, she just took to the streets like you see her now. I think that she may be a strange woman, a sad woman, but she's not crazy."

"Mom and Dad, did you know this?" Sarah asks.

"Well, we knew that she was a recluse, but I never heard the story about her plans to wed. That was so long ago." Mrs. Wright looks at her husband waiting for his response.

"Yeah, Liz is right. We never heard the story about the Bentons. You see people who seem to have given up on life and they just disappear into the background." Mr. Wright has a look of concern.

"Didn't she have any family?" Sarah asks Mrs. Costello whose wheelchair is now looking more like a throne as she has everyone's undivided attention.

"Yes, she did have a couple of Aunts and Uncles, but they were much older and all deceased now, I'm afraid. One cousin that she was very close to was much younger. Ella was what I called her. A cute little girl who was very close to Bell as she lost her own Mother, Bell's Aunt, at a very young age. But after the death of Bell's young man she distanced herself from everyone including Ella. She retreated from life." Mrs. Costello sips her drink.

"So, are you saying that you think she's living in that mansion?" John asks.

"My guess would be that she is. Of course, there is that lovely home that her beloved built. It's on the property, you know." Mrs. Costello extends her hand with her cup. "Just cranberry juice, dear."

Sarah takes the cup. "The house that he built is on the property? Where?" she prods.

"Oh, way in the back. It's a big piece of property, that Benton place. He built it right on the Benton land. It'd be hard to see I suspect, with the overgrowth and all. But, it's in the back of the mansion, way back and hidden in the woods."

Sarah is stunned and turns to the table that holds the beverages. She fills up Mrs. Costello's cup and quickly steps back to hand it to her.

"Sarah," John says looking intently at her.

"I know! We need to go out there tomorrow!" Sarah looks at her parents. "Mom, where would you go if you were sad and withdrawn?"

"I think we both know," Mrs. Wright answers. "It wouldn't be in that big mansion."

"Exactly! That would explain why no one's stepped foot anywhere near the mansion," Sarah exclaims.

"I guess I know what we're doing in the morning." John turns around and takes a cookie off a plate on the dining room table behind him.

"Yes, and we'll be lucky to get out there with this snow coming down." Sarah takes a deep breath. "Wow." She leans down and kisses Mrs. Costello on her forehead. "Thank you for sharing that, Mrs. Costello."

"Of course, Sarah. I didn't realize that it was of such value." She looks at Sarah and furrows her brow. "Exactly why is it, dear? Of value? I'm still not clear."

"Sarah's trying find out where Bell and Emma might be. I think that may have given a clue to solving a big mystery," Mr. Wright adds.

"Oh! Well, I'm glad!" Mrs. Costello smiles and takes a sip of her cranberry juice.

John leans over and kisses her cheek. "Thank you, Mrs. Costello."
"For what, dear?" Mrs. Costello asks.
"For giving me back my wife for the night," he shares.
"Happy to help out. Happy to help," she responds.

Chapter Nine
Hidden Treasure

The snow continues to come down in large clumps as predicted, and accumulates quickly. Sarah steps onto the rotted front porch. The wood planks creak and buckle as she carefully makes her way to the front door of the neglected home. Peeled paint litters the porch and surrounding area where the pillars have expelled the cracked debris, no longer useful to the rotting wood.

She steps up to the door in anticipation of what may lie behind it. Sarah takes the tarnished knocker in her hand, the Lion looking even more fierce, his face blackened. She pulls it up and releases it, sounding a hollow bang throughout the empty interior.

Again, there is silence. She raises it again and releases. The bang echoes and then stops. Then there is a noise. A shuffling. Footsteps? No. It sounds more like an animal. Perhaps a raccoon that has made its way into the home.

"I shouldn't have come," Sarah whispers and turns to face the road, stepping off of the porch. "There isn't anyone here. No one could inhabit this place."

"Wait," John says, walking up behind her. "Listen." They are silent and suddenly hear a shuffling and then sniffing.

"That's an animal," Sarah whispers as she tiptoes to the door and places her ear on it. "There it is again! Yeah, that's a small animal. Not human for sure."

"I think that we should go in." John gives her a look of confidence and determination.

"John, I don't know about that. It doesn't seem right to just walk in." She steps back as though preparing to leave.

"Right or wrong, we need to find out what's going on, Sarah. We decided, remember? It's the only way to find out. You can stay here, but I'm going in." John steps forward and places his hand on the door knob. He kicks away a drift of snow that has settled against the door, takes a big breath and slowly turns it. They hear a scampering that echoes in the interior. "Well, it's not locked." John turns the knob until it stops and then gives the door a push. It doesn't give in easily.

Sarah takes a deep breath and covers her mouth with both hands in anticipation of what they will find.

"Sarah, it's O.K. Relax!" John pushes harder, and the door gives way as it scrapes across the warped floor. It opens wide, creaking until it stops. The light hits the entrance, creating beams of dust in the dark foyer. Directly ahead is a large, wooden staircase lined with a worn antique carpet. Sarah and John pause and look at each other, saying nothing.

John cautiously steps in. The floor creaks loudly. He turns and looks at Sarah, waving her in. "Come on. It's fine. No one's here."

"So far." Sarah doesn't budge.

"Yeah, the floors are covered with dust. I can see paw prints and that's about it."

"John, there could be an angry animal in there." Sarah steps forward.

"They're small prints. Probably a raccoon." He looks at Sarah. "It's already gone. It's more afraid than we are." He waves her in. "Seriously, Sarah, get in here! We need to make sure."

Sarah steps forward. The floor creaks as she enters the foyer. She gasps.

"What?" John stops.

"It's just like my dream! Look! Look to the left. The pocket doors! There's a chandelier in that room and heavy burgundy drapes." Sarah points.

"Geez, you scared me. I thought you saw the raccoon!" He quietly laughs. "Let's check the rooms." John walks down the hallway past the staircase stepping into each room along the way until he reaches the back of the mansion. He opens each door, examining rooms that have been untouched for decades. "Looks like a sitting room," he says as he opens two large, solid French doors. He stands in the hallway and looks around its interior. "Rob was right. No one's stepped in here for years."

Sarah walks in back of John like a shadow. They both shuffle down the hall further. Sarah tightly grasps his jacket with one hand and places her other on his shoulder.

"Sarah," John whispers.

"What?" She stops and stiffens.

"You're digging your nails into my shoulder."

"Oh. Sorry. This is just so intense! I feel like we're trespassing!" She takes her hand off of his shoulder.

"That's because we *are* trespassing. Relax! No one is in this house. Look at the dust. It's thick. It hasn't been disturbed for ages." He points to the surfaces and floors covered with thick grime and debris.

"You're right. So why are we whispering and tip toeing?" Sarah whispers.

John pauses, turns and looks at her. "I don't know." They look at one another for a moment and then quietly laugh. "O.K., let's relax." He grabs her hand. "Come on." He leads her through the house. They slowly examine the dark, dusty rooms. One by one, each displays antique furnishings, carpets and draperies all in place as though the home was suddenly deserted. The kitchen is stocked with beautiful place settings, glassware and cookware stacked in cupboards. A large pantry is filled with food now decayed. Glass jars reveal various contents that are now colorless and petrified. Cans are rusted and bulging; ready to explode.

The couple stands in the kitchen staring at their surroundings, frozen in time. "This is bizarre." Sarah shakes her head in amazement. "What do you think happened?"

"Who can say? A broken heart." John looks at Sarah with sad eyes.

"But where is she? All of this is hers." Sarah slowly shakes her head.

"Obviously it doesn't mean anything to her." John continues to stare at Sarah.

Sarah squints her eyes and looks at the floor. The small animal prints lead to a doggy door cut into the kitchen door. She studies the paw prints. "This house is a hangout for wild animals and dust. This *doesn't* mean anything to her," she turns and looks at John, "but that other house does. Mrs. Costello said that it's at the back of the property. It's in the woods. We probably can't even see it." She grabs John's hand. "Come on. She's not here. We need to find that other home!"

Sarah leads him out the back door. The animal prints leave a trail in the snow and lead through the backyard to the edge of the property where a dense woods begins.

"There! Look at the paw prints! We need to follow them!" Sarah walks briskly with John close behind.

They finally reach the end of the cleared property where a thick woods begins. Sarah pushes down and parts twigs, carefully following the direction of the animal prints. "Let me take the lead, Sarah." John steps in front of her and begins to push down the heavy brush, stepping on big branches with his feet. He makes a path as they continue to battle through. After several minutes, they hear a bark.

"Shhhh." Sarah says. They stop and are silent. Again, they hear a bark. "John, the prints. Do you think that's Emma?"

"We'll find out. Look." John points at what appears to be a small building, barely seen through the trees that surround them. "That has to be it." He pushes through further with Sarah close behind. Their jackets and pants are covered with burrs, sticks and dead leaves.

Finally, they come upon a clearing and in the middle sits a beautiful, stone cottage looking like something out of a fairy tale, but with years of neglect. Overgrown vines have claimed the exterior and moss grows on the roof.

"Oh my gosh!" Sarah gasps. They stand and stare in total amazement. "This is the house. The one that Mrs. Costello told us about. He built it for her!" Sarah turns to John. "This beautiful home. They never got to live in it together."

John points. "Sarah, look! Emma!" Standing at the front of the house is Emma, wagging her tail. She barks once again.

"She knows you," Sarah says. "Bell must be in there." She turns and looks at John. "Should we?"

"Yes, Sarah. We have to do this." John steps forward and onto the front, stone stoop. He stands at the door and turns to look at Sarah. "Come on. It'll be O.K."

Sarah joins him and takes a deep breath. John knocks while Emma continues to wag her tail, looking up at John as though she has something to tell. There is silence. John knocks again.

"She doesn't live here, either," Sarah says. She steps away from the door and pushes thorny bushes away in an attempt to get close enough to look in one of the windows.

"Oh, I think she does," John says, pointing to the ground. There, along with their footprints and Emma's are a fourth set of prints that lead from the porch to a trail which has obviously been used many times.

"Do you think she's in there?" Sarah stares at the footprints.

"Bell doesn't go anywhere without this dog. I have to go in." John looks for confirmation. Sarah nods her head in agreement and John pushes his thumb down on the door handle latch. It clicks loudly.

The two step into the entrance which opens directly into a living room where a large, wood fireplace stands. Surrounding it are two beautiful stuffed, French style arm chairs with a small table in between, and on the other side, an oversized love seat. A beautiful, pale blue Persian carpet is laid in the center of the room. Matching pillows adorn the sofa and several table lamps are placed around on various antique tables. On the mantel are several black and white framed photos and over it, an expensive French gilded mirror. The room is warm and clean.

Sarah and John stand in silence and look at one another wondering what their next move will be. Sarah points to the hallway off of the living area and John leads the way with her close behind. The wide wood plank floor is polished and unmarked. Not a creak is heard as they walk on it. Within a few feet, John comes to a door that is slightly open. He knocks on it and hears nothing.

"Ms. Benton? Miss Bell?" Sarah announces as she steps forward and slowly pushes the door open.

Suddenly, Emma bolts ahead of them and runs into the room. She heads toward a bed in the corner and jumps on it. The room is dark. It appears that there is someone in the bed and the couple have no doubts as to who it might be.

"Bell?" Sarah calls out and walks toward the bed. "Miss Benton?" She steps to the edge of the bed and places her hand on the large mound of comforters and blankets.

They hear a mumbling come from the thick comforter and it moves. Sarah grasps the top of the blankets and pulls it down to reveal a face. There, buried under the pile of down is Bell who appears to be asleep.

Sarah places her hand on the old lady's forehead. "John, she's burning up! We need to call an ambulance."

"I'm on it," John replies, pulling out his cell phone. He quickly dials emergency.

"Bell?" Sarah takes Bell's hand in hers and pats it, attempting to get her to respond. "Can you hear me? If you can hear me, squeeze my hand." There is no response. Bell then moans and Emma, standing on the bed with her front paws on Bell's arm, barks.

"John, who knows how long she's been here like this. Can you please check to see if Emma has water, and please bring a glass of water in here for Bell?" Sarah sits on the bed, still holding Bell's hand

and strokes it. "Bell, you're going to be fine. Help is on the way." Bell moans again.

"Bell, John and I are going to take care of Emma until you get well. Don't worry about that." Suddenly, the frail woman opens her eyes slightly and looks at Sarah and smiles. She closes them again and appears to lose consciousness.

"Oh Bell," Sarah strokes her face.

John appears with a glass of water and a cold wash cloth. "I brought this to cool her down until the ambulance gets here. "It's hard to say how long she's been like this, but Emma's water bowl was empty. Here." John hands Sarah the water and the wash cloth.

"She doesn't seem to be conscious. I don't think she's even able to sit up to drink the water. The medics will hydrate her immediately. Bell, hang in there! Help is on the way." Sarah lays the cloth on Bell's forehead and holds it with her hand.

"Oh John, I'm so worried," Sarah whispers.

"It'll be O.K." John rubs Sarah's shoulder to comfort her. They both watch Bell, feeling helpless.

Soon, the Medics arrive and phone John's cell. John instructs them on how to reach the remote home and they soon appear with a cot so that they can carry Bell back to the ambulance, parked at the mansion. Sarah and John watch them take Bell's vital signs and administer an I.V. before placing her frail little body on the cot in preparation to carry her out.

"Is she going to be O.K.?" Sarah asks, following them to the front door.

"She has a pretty high fever and she's dehydrated. She most likely has pneumonia and at her age it carries a big risk. We'll know more when we get her to the hospital where she can get chest X-rays and re-hydrate. It's a good thing that you found her. She's barely conscious," the medic shares.

John puts his arm around Sarah as they watch Bell get carried back through the woods and to the ambulance. With all of the commotion at the house, in an instance it is silent. Sarah turns to John and they hug.

"I'm so worried about her." Sarah says as John continues to hold her.

"I am too," John responds and then looks around the room. "Wait. Where's Emma? I made sure that she didn't go out that front door!"

The two quickly part and begin to scour the home. "Emma!" Sarah shouts as she gets on her hands and knees looking under the sofa and chairs.

"She's in here!" John shouts. "She's under the bed!"

Sarah joins John in the bedroom and sees him pulling Emma out from under the bed. "Oh, the poor baby! All of the excitement and people here, and seeing her Mama being taken away must have frightened her terribly!" Sarah leans over to pet Emma who is cowering in John's arms, shaking.

"Let's get her back to our place. We need to get food and water in her." They search around for Emma's belongings and find a small doggy bed and toys.

Sarah steps onto the front porch, looking at the cottage. "It must have been beautiful once," she says to herself. She proceeds to step down when she sees something protruding out of the snow on the side of the porch. She leans down, pulls off her gloves and searches around in the pile of snow and feels that it is a piece of metal. She brushes off the snow and sees that is gold in color and deeply tarnished.

"John, take a look at this," Sarah says, as she continues to clear the snow and dirt that is packed around the object. John steps onto the porch, still holding Emma. Sarah takes both hands and pulls on the metal piece until she dislodges it, sending dirt and snow everywhere.

"What is it?" John asks.

"It's a bell." Sarah takes her glove and clears off the snow and dirt. "Bell Cottage," she says as she reads the words etched into the tarnished surface. "It must have been made for the cottage. A dedication." She looks at John. "Look." Sarah points to a metal hangar on the side of the house just to the right of the entrance. "It belongs there, would be my guess."

"Pretty sweet," he says.

"And romantic," Sarah adds. "Come on. Let's get Emma back and I'll bring this with us."

They close up the cottage and the two make their way back through the brush and to their car. John holds the still trembling Emma and hands her off to Sarah who consoles the frightened dog on their way home.

"Looks like Baxter is O.K. with a visitor," John comments as they enter to the happy pup, placing Emma on the floor. Baxter sniffs Emma who cautious steps back then moves forward and sniffs Baxter's face. Her tail begins to wag. "That's a good sign," John smiles. "I'll go get Emma fed if you let Baxter out."

"Absolutely." The two walk to the kitchen where John begins to prepare a dinner and water bowl for Emma. In the meantime, Baxter is anxious to explore the backyard and bolts when Sarah opens the kitchen door.

"I'm still in shock," Sarah says, as she sits down at the kitchen table. "This is so much to take in. I'd like to head over to the hospital as soon as we get the dogs situated."

"Agreed." John opens a can of dog food and spoons it into a bowl, chopping it up. He places it on the floor and Emma doesn't miss a moment before scarfing it down. They watch the hungry dog. "Who knows how long she's gone without food. It's a good thing that she has extra padding on her." The dog quickly finishes her dinner and laps up the entire bowl of water. John replenishes it. Little Emma lays down, panting heavily and wags her tail as she watches the two.

"She's so sweet," Sarah says as she leans down and pets the dog. Emma is receptive to the attention. "Emma, we'll do our best to take care of your Mommy. Don't you worry, Sweetie." Emma looks at Sarah with innocent eyes.

"I'll let Baxter in." John opens the kitchen door to Baxter who is covered in snow. He shakes, flipping it all over the kitchen. John grabs a towel and wipes him down. "Good boy, Bax!"

John, smiling, looks up to see that tears are welling up in Sarah's eyes. "Oh honey, don't worry. Emma's safe now. Let's go check on Bell. It's going to be O.K." John stands and gives Sarah a hug.

"I know," Sarah holds John close. "It's a lot to take in. She's so alone!"

"Not any more. We're here for her. Come on. The dogs are taken care of. Let's get our coats on and get over to the hospital."

John grabs Sarah's hand and leads her into the living room where they bundle up and head to the car. The snow ceases to fall and they safely make their way to their destination.

Chapter Ten
A Tall Order

"Bell Benton?" the hospital receptionist asks as John and Sarah watch her search through the computer database.

"Yes. She was just admitted through emergency," Sarah explains.

"Are you family?" the woman asks.

The two look at one another. "Yes. Yes, we are," Sarah responds.

"Here. Please sign in. Here are your passes." The woman hands them two cards imprinted with their names and directs them to the third floor intensive care unit.

They make their way up the elevate and to the room where they find Bell in an oxygen tent. A physician stands by, writing on a clipboard. "Hello. Are you the ones that found Miss Bell here?" he asks.

"Yes," John answers. "Is she going to be O.K.?"

"Well, she just came out of X-ray and it looks like she has pneumonia. Her fever is high and she's dehydrated. But, we're taking care of that. It will take a few hours to get fluids back into her. She's responding to them already which is good." He looks at his notes. "May we step into the hall?" The three step into the hallway where he looks up from his clipboard. "It's going to be a long night. She has a lot of fluid in her lungs and we need to get her temperature down. With her age and the stroke," he continues.

"Wait, excuse me? Did you say the stroke? She had a stroke too?" Sarah asks.

"Not recently. She had a stroke at some point prior to the pneumonia." The doctor looks at them both. "Didn't you know that? It's why she shuffles and slurs her words." He examines their faces, waiting for a response. "I'm surprised that this didn't trigger another one."

"Oh my gosh," John says, looking down at the floor and placing his hand on his forehead. "The mumbling, lack of eye contact, the shuffling. Why didn't we see this?" He looks at Sarah.

"It's so simple." Sarah gives a big sigh and shakes her head. "No wonder she isn't communicating with anyone. She can't."

"My guess is that this has gone untreated for some time," the doctor states. "She may have been able to recover her speech and mobility with therapy."

"Is it too late?" John asks.

"It's never too late," the doctor responds. "Our first priority is to stabilize her. We'll know more by tomorrow, *if* she makes it through the night." He looks at John and Sarah with compassion.

"It's that bad?" Sarah asks.

"I'm afraid with pneumonia and her current condition, it is definitely a critical situation. The dehydration and fever are my biggest concern at the moment."

John extends his hand. "Doctor, we appreciate all that you've done. We're going to stay here a while if that's O.K."

"You're family. You can stay as long as you'd like." He shakes John's hand and then Sarah's. "If you have any questions, I'll be on duty all night. Just ask for Doctor David Johnson," he smiles. "I'll be checking on Bell frequently and we'll keep you updated."

"Thank you, doctor," Sarah says. The doctor spends a few more minutes checking on Bell's vitals and medications before leaving.

John and Sarah sit in Bell's room in silence. They watch her as she breaths steadily, but shallow. Sarah gets up and fumbles in her purse. She pulls the Christmas star out and shows it to John.

"For good luck," she says as she hangs the star from the frame that holds up the oxygen tent. She releases it and it dangles, turning and dazzling as the dim hospital room lights reflect off of it.

"I remember that star," John smiles. They sit and watch as Bell's monitor slowly bleeps in a rhythmic pattern.

"John, I'm thinking." Sarah turns to him and smiles. "Now don't make any jokes."

John smiles back. "I promise. Go ahead."

"Well, Bell's cousin Ella was very close to her. Mrs. Costello said that she was very young at the time, so she wouldn't be that old now. I know that this may be a stretch, but we don't know if Bell's going to make it through the night. Wouldn't it be worth trying to find her and let her know about the situation?"

"Now why would I make a joke about that? I think that's an awesome idea, but where do we start?" John watches Bell's breathing monitors.

"I don't know. I just don't know." Sarah looks off into blank space thinking. A few minutes pass. "Oh my gosh!"

John looks at her, his eyebrows raised. "What?"

"Mrs. Costello. She knew Ella. Remember what she shared at the holiday party? You know how she is. You have to prod her for information. We need to find out where Ella could possibly be. She may be the only relative who's alive and cares about Bell."

"It's getting late," John reminds Sarah.

"Bell's life may be slipping away. It's not too late!" Sarah stands and grabs John's hand. "Come on, we're going to make a surprise visit to Mrs. Costello!"

"Children! What on earth?! Come in! Come in!" Mrs. Costello stands at the door with her walker.

"We apologize Mrs. Costello. We wouldn't barge in like this so late if it wasn't urgent," Sarah says as she enters the house.

"Urgent? My goodness! Now don't you worry about me. I was up watching one of my T.V. programs. You two come in and take a seat in the living room and tell me what's so important." Mrs. Costello shuffles with her walker back to her recliner that is parked next to a window overlooking the street. "Should we get your parents over here?"

"No, it's not something that my parents can help with. You're the only one that we know that may be able to help," Sarah states as she and John take their seats on the living room sofa.

"This sounds quite serious. You have me concerned now. Are you sick?" she asks.

"No, but *someone* is sick and we need to ask you some questions. It's old lady . . . it's Bell Benton. She's in the hospital in critical condition with pneumonia and frankly, we don't know if she'll make it through the night," John says. "You see, we found her at her home, unconscious."

"Oh, that's terrible! I'm so sorry to hear that! God bless her! But, how can I help?" Mrs. Costello is riveted.

"You mentioned that you knew Bell's cousin, Ella. She seems to be the only family that Bell has and the only person that we can reach out to. With Bell's condition, time is of the essence." Sarah scoots to the edge of the couch. "Mrs. Costello, where can we find Ella?"

"Oh, goodness, Sarah, that's been such a long time ago. Why did you come to ask me?" Mrs. Costello looks confused.

"Because you were the only one that seemed to know about Bell's past and her family connections," Sarah reminds her. "We thought that you may have an idea about where Ella may live or how we could get in touch with her."

"Oh Sarah, Ella left Rosedale a long ago. She was such a sweet, young gal. Lost her Mother at a young age you know," Mrs. Costello replies.

"Yes, I remember, you told us. They were very close at one time, right?" Sarah asks.

"Oh yes, very close. Did everything together. That little Ella followed Bell around like a pup. That was, until we all lost Bell to her sadness. She didn't give Ella much attention after that and then Ella got older and eventually moved away. But if you want to know about

Ella, you should ask Joe Conner. Joe can tell you much more about her than I can," she gives a weak smile.

"Judge Joe? What would Judge Joe know about Ella?" John asks.

"Well, he used to date her when they were young. They were engaged at one time. They were quite an item. I don't know if they stayed in touch through the years, but he would have a better idea of where she might be than I would." Mrs. Costello pauses, looking at the two. "You knew that, right?"

"Gabby? That's Gabby?" John asks. "Gabby, the love of his life is Bell's cousin Ella?"

"Why yes. Her name is Gabriella, but we called her Ella when she was a little girl. Gabriella or Gabby to most others. Her father insisted that she go off to art school and the two broke up and never got back together. You know how it goes when you're young. Time and distance can pull people apart. She had some wonderful travels through her art, overseas and all. As I understand it, she ended up getting married. It broke Joe's heart. God bless him, he never found anyone after he lost his Gabby. Life just takes us in different directions sometimes. You never know why, but everything has a purpose." Mrs. Costello gets a peaceful look on her face.

"This is amazing," Sarah says, shaking her head. "Absolutely amazing."

"Unbelievable," John looks at Sarah in disbelief. "So, Mrs. Costello, are you saying that we should go over there and ask him about this now?" John asks.

"Absolutely. If you're saying that Bell may not make it through the night, I think that Gabby would want to know. That is, if you can find her. This may be her chance to reunite with Bell. That Bell can be stubborn. She hasn't allowed anyone into her life for a very long time, but she's a good woman. She was like a Mother to Gabby when she needed her family's love. This could be the chance she has been looking for to have Bell back in her life." She pauses. "Yes, go see Joe right now and if he objects, you tell him that Stella told you that it was O.K."

John and Sarah stand, still in shock. "I guess we have another surprise visit to make," John announces.

"Oh boy, this is going to be interesting!" Sarah makes a face. "Mrs. Costello, I'm so sorry to have bothered you. We appreciate you allowing us to come into your home. This has been so helpful."

"It's fine! I'm glad that I could help and I will pray that Bell recovers. Bless you both for caring!" Mrs. Costello starts to get up from her chair.

"No, no!" John says, gently placing his hand on her shoulder to stop her. "You stay right in that chair and we'll let ourselves out. Have a nice night and thank you again." John kisses Mrs. Costello on the forehead and she giggles.

"Yes, thank you, Mrs. Costello. We'll let you know how everything turns out." Sarah walks to her and kisses her cheek before walking to the front door.

John and Sarah exit the home and stand on the front porch, looking out to the street. It is dark and the Christmas decorations on the surrounding homes are lit, creating a colorful, soft glow on the crystalized snow. Mrs. Costello watches from her window as the couple leaves and waves at them. She pushes pack in her recliner. "Poor old Bell," she says to herself, shaking her head. "Poor old Bell."

John and Sarah pull up to the stately brick Tudor home. Sarah sees that interior lights are lit. "Well, it looks like he's up," she says as they pull onto the pebble drive, now coated with a thin sheet of ice.

The trees in the front yard are loaded with white, twinkling holiday lights that illuminate the front lawn. They head up the newly shoveled walkway and to a wooden arched door with a small window for peeking out. John takes a deep breath, his exhale visible in the cold air, and knocks. Footsteps can be heard and shortly, a face appears in the small window. It is Judge Joe with a look of surprise. He opens the door.

"Now what in the heck are you two doing here on this frosty night?

Come in, come in!" He is dressed in a deep red, velvet robe. His feet are tucked into brown leather slippers lined with lamb's wool, and he holds a crystal glass filled with port. He directs them to a side room with a fireplace that is blazing. In front of it is a sofa with newspapers and magazines stacked and scattered on it.

"I was just catching up on some reading. May I offer you a port?" Judge Joe raises his glass.

"I'd love one," Sarah says, looking at John who raises his eyebrows. "What? After today, I could use a drink! Besides, you're driving!"

"Hey, go ahead. You're right. One of us needs a stiff drink," John agrees.

The Judge walks to a mahogany bar located in the corner in front of a full wall of shelves packed with books. The entire room is covered with mahogany paneling, and decorated with masculine furnishings. An entire wall of floor to ceiling windows, flanked with heavy draperies overlooks the front yard.

"Now, something tells me that this isn't just a social call," he says as he pulls the glass stopper off of a decanter. He pulls out a crystal glass and gives a good pour before handing it to Sarah.

"Thanks." Sarah accepts the glass, takes a big swig and gives a satisfying sigh. "You're right. As much as we love you, we're not here to socialize," Sarah admits.

"Oh, now this sounds serious," the Judge says and walks to the sofa, taking a seat. He pushes a stack of magazines aside and pats the place beside him. "Sarah, bring your port with you and come sit down. John, take a seat in the chair. Tell me what you kids have come here to discuss."

"First of all, we want to apologize for barging in like this so late and unannounced, but Judge Joe, we wouldn't have come over here if it wasn't important. You see, Bell has taken ill. John and I found her in the house in the back of the Benton property, unconscious and with a fever." Sarah scoots onto the sofa.

"Oh no. I was afraid that something like this would happen." The Judge looks off into the fire, thinking to himself.

"She's in the hospital now, getting the best care. We don't know how long she was lying there like that, or just how severe her pneumonia is. If she makes it through the night, we'll be grateful. The doctors weren't sure," John adds.

The Judge shakes his head. "Bell is a stubborn woman. Always was."

"Judge Joe, I want to ask you something and if John and I are overstepping our boundaries, you just tell us and we'll be gone." Sarah takes a deep breath and another swig of port. "Mrs. Costello shared with us that your former girlfriend Gabby is, well, Gabriella, Bell's cousin. Is that true?" Sarah stares at Judge Joe who is still gazing into the fire, deep in thought.

"Gabriella. Gabby." He pauses and smiles. "My Gabby. Yes. Yes, indeed she is related to Bell. They used to be the closest of friends, despite their age difference." The Judge stands and walks to the bar, uncorking the port stopper. "You see, Gabriella's mother had died when she was a baby and Bell really took to her. They're cousins, but Bell was also a good friend and a mother figure. They certainly were thick as thieves those two." He splashes more port into his glass and places the stopper back into the decanter. "Always having fun and being silly." He pauses again for a very long time, staring back into the fire and takes a sip of port. "That's when Bell was full of joy. Childlike, she was. She had so much hope and love in her." He stops and turns toward them. "Then Prescott died."

Sarah sits up straight and shoots her gaze toward John. "Prescott? Do you mean Bell's fiancé?"

"Yes. Prescott was a young man when he had his accident." The Judge looks at Sarah with a sympathetic smile.

"I had a dream about him, a man named Prescott! He and Bell were together!" Sarah speaks quickly and is out of breath.

John watches her. "It's true. Sarah had a dream." John shakes his head as though trying to clear it, in disbelief.

"I have the star again, Judge Joe. I can't explain it, but I think it had something to do with a dream that I had!" Sarah looks at the Judge, waiting for answers.

"Oh, you got the star back, did you? It wields real power, Sarah." The Judge walks to the fireplace and rests his hand on the mantle.

"Judge Joe, what happened to Gabriella?" John asks.

"My Gabby." He smiles. "She was young when Prescott died and Bell went into a very deep depression. No one could reach her. You know the story by now. She became a recluse. The once vibrant woman was gone, and she shut everyone out, including Gabby." The Judge throws a log on the fire and walks to the sofa, taking a seat.

"When Gabriella was accepted to a prestigious art school on the east coast, her Father picked up and moved there. I know that she had attempted to contact Bell many times, but Bell wouldn't have it. Bell has chosen to live in isolation and there's nothing against the law that says that she can't," the Judge states.

"But, we didn't find her in the mansion. She's living in the small cottage on the back of the property," Sarah adds.

"The home that Prescott built for them before his death." The Judge nods. "A beautiful cottage at one time. I'm not surprised."

"But, Judge Joe, why didn't you tell us all of this?" Sarah asks.

The Judge looks closely at Sarah and smiles. "I know how much you love a good mystery. In all honesty, I really didn't have all of the answers for you, Sarah, and it didn't occur to me that Bell would be living in that cottage. It got swallowed up in the woods years ago. I think that all that has occurred is a message that it's time for things to change." He pauses. "How can I help?"

"Well, considering that Gabriella is her only known, closest relative, we thought that you could help us find her. I'm sure she'd want to know that Bell's in the hospital. Maybe there's a chance to bring them back together and let Bell know that she's not alone." Sarah looks at John with a worried expression. "Maybe it'll bring some joy back into her life."

The Judge stands up and strokes his chin. "That's a tall order, but I'll make a few calls." He turns to the two. "I don't know what Gabby's life is like at this point in time, but I don't doubt that she would welcome the opportunity to reunite with Bell. I'll do my best."

Sarah leaps up, almost spilling her port. "Oh thank you!" She places the glass down on a table and throws her arms around him.

"O.K., O.K., Sarah!" He gives her a big hug. "You are one enthusiastic young lady!" He takes her shoulders and looks her in the eyes. "You are also a very caring, selfless young person. John! That includes you. You saved a life today."

"Hopefully," John says, standing. "We'll know more in the next 24 to 48 hours."

Sarah looks at the Judge, her face softens. "Judge Joe, I know that Gabby has moved on with her life, but maybe this was meant to be. Maybe it will bring joy into your life too."

Judge Joe smiles and looks back into the fire. "That was a long time ago, Sarah. That time has passed. But if Bell and Gabby find their way back to one another, that will be all the joy I need." He turns and looks at Sarah with a peaceful expression. "I'm grateful to be here, in this wonderful town, and with wonderful people like you Sarah, and John, and your parents. You're my family. I'm content."

Sarah gives him another hug. "We'll always be your family and we're so fortunate to have you in our lives."

"O.K., you two. Go get some rest. Tomorrow is going to be a long day if we're going to get Bell back to good health. This will be our chance to get things in order before, God willing, that stubborn, old lady is back in action!"

Judge Joe walks Sarah and John to the front door and waves good bye as they make their way back to their home. Standing at the door waiting is Baxter along with Emma who joins in the happy greeting.

Chapter Eleven
Emma to the Rescue

Sarah awakens to the ringing of her cell phone. She is in a deep sleep and struggles to answer it in time. "Hello?" She rubs her eyes and tries to see where the call is coming from.

"Sarah, it's Joe. Get dressed and bring Emma with you to the hospital."

"Is everything O.K.? Did Bell take a turn for the worse?" Sarah sits up straight in her bed.

"She's still in critical condition. I think if you bring Emma, it might perk her up. I got permission from the hospital. Can you get here within the hour?" the Judge asks.

"Of course," Sarah answers. "We'll see you there as soon as we can." Sarah hangs up, places her hand on John's shoulder and shakes him. "John! Wake up. Bell's still in critical condition and Judge Joe wants us to bring Emma to her room. He thinks it'll help her to recover, and I agree. We need to get dressed and over there."

John turns over and looks at Sarah with one eye open. "O.K., honey. Can you make the coffee while I shower?"

"John, you don't have time to shower! Throw on some jeans. I'm going to feed Baxter and Emma and we're going straight to the hospital. Now get a move on!" She smacks his butt.

The two quickly dress and head to the kitchen where they get the dogs ready. Sarah grabs one of Baxter's red bandanas and ties it around Emma's neck. She wags her tail as though pleased. They place leashes on the dogs and load them in the car before heading to the hospital.

"We're here to see Bell Benton," Sarah says to the hospital receptionist, waiting to explain the reason why two dogs accompany them.

"Bell Benton." The receptionist looks over the counter and down at the dogs, and smiles. "Yes, Judge Conner told us to expect an extra fuzzy visitor." She pauses. "Or two, I see."

"Yes, this is Emma's cousin, Baxter," John adds.

"Oh, they're cousins. Well then we can't separate cousins. Just make sure they stay with you at all times." The woman smiles again and leans down to pet them. She takes a tag and slips it on each dog's collar. "Just in case anyone asks, show them the doggy pass."

John and Sarah thank her and head to Bell's room. They quietly enter and see Judge Joe sitting next to her bedside. Bell's eyes are closed and she remains in the oxygen tent. The star hangs at the end of the bed, dazzling.

"Welcome," Judge Joe whispers. "The doctor will be here in a moment. He's going to open the tent up so that Emma can lay next to Bell."

Sarah nods and leans down to pet and calm Emma who is excited to see her owner.

The doctor soon appears and looks down at the dogs. "I understand that we have a special visitor for Ms. Bell!" He leans down and pets Emma, then Baxter.

"This is Emma, Bell's baby. Thank you so much for allowing us to bring her in," Sarah says.

"It's my pleasure. Bell isn't out of the danger zone, but I can't see any harm in letting her spend time with her pup. Maybe it can bring her out of this. It's worth a try." He walks to the oxygen tent and opens up a sealed seam. "Bell isn't in any risk of infection, so if you bring Emma over here, we can place her on the bed."

John picks up the portly dog and gently lifts her onto the bed. Emma carefully lays next to Bell, gently placing her head on Bell's shoulder as though knowing of her frail condition. She gives Bell a small lick on the face.

"Can she stay here for a while?" Sarah asks.

"As long as she stays still, she's fine. Just make sure that she isn't walking around on the bed and interfering with Bell's IV," the doctor says. "Considering the circumstances, I think that this will do more good than harm. Animals can have a very positive effect on people, and I know that Emma is everything to Bell. Let's hope this boosts her system so that she can battle the pneumonia."

"We'll keep a close eye on her," John promises. "It looks like Emma is content just being here."

"Yes, it appears so." The doctor turns to Judge Joe who is still sitting near the bedside. "Judge Conner, good to see you. I'll be back to check on Bell shortly. I'm sure all of you will keep an eye on her and notify the nurses if there is anything you need."

"David, we appreciate all that you're doing." Judge Joe stands and shakes the doctor's hand. Doctor Johnson bids them farewell and is off to his next patient.

Judge Joe walks over to Sarah and John. "There's something else." He smiles.

"You found Gabriella?" Sarah holds back excitement.

"Better." He raises one eyebrow.

"Better than finding Gabriella? What could be better?" John asks.

"Flying her here to be with Bell in person," he responds.

"What?" Sarah looks confused. The Judge points to the door and a stout woman walks in. Her hair, now more grey than blond, is pulled up into a twist and her skin is flawless and shines. She enters the room with a big smile.

"Hello. I'm Bell's cousin, Gabby." She extends her hand to Sarah.

"Forget the handshake," Sarah says pulling her in and giving her a big hug. "How? When?"

"Oh, it took a few calls, but when I got to Gabby, she insisted on flying in immediately. She arrived early this morning," the Judge shares.

"Yes. I'm so thankful to Joe for getting me here so that I can be with

Bell. And I want to thank you both from the bottom of my heart. I understand that you took the time to check on her and if you hadn't, Bell wouldn't be here. I can't begin to tell you how much this all means to me!"

"So, you were already here at the hospital?" John asks.

"Yes, I flew in and Joe brought me here straight from the airport. I've been with Bell a couple of hours. I wanted to give you all a moment to introduce Emma back to Bell, so I went down to grab a cup of coffee." She smiles at Judge Joe. "We wanted to surprise you."

"It certainly is a surprise! You must be exhausted!" Sarah says.

"I'm a bit tired, but I've been waiting for this opportunity my whole life. It's time that Bell let her family back in and allow someone to finally take care of her. There will be no more street roaming or hiding in that cottage. Things are going to change." She walks in the room and takes a seat.

"Bell is a stubborn and guarded woman. Will she allow that?" Sarah asks.

"Yes, I know that better than anyone. She isn't going to have a choice. Bell's older and she needs care. She may object, but it's going to happen. If she pulls out of this, we're going to get her strong and into therapy so that she can speak again." Gabby looks at Bell and Emma, cuddling as they both sleep.

"Gabriella, are you saying that you're going to be staying here in Rosedale?" John looks surprised.

"Please, John. Call me Gabby. Yes, I'll be here in Rosedale," she looks over at Judge Joe.

The Judge smiles at her. "You see, Gabby and I had a very long chat. We have a lot of years and a lot of memories that we've missed."

"And need to catch up on," Gabby smiles.

Sarah has a sheepish smile. "Uh, I'm not exactly sure what you're saying, but do I sense a reunion of some kind here?" She catches herself and realizes how presumptuous she sounds. "Oh, I'm sorry! I don't mean to be so nosey."

"Well, I've been on my own for a few years. I'd be close to Bell and can take care of her, God willing that she pulls through this. I'm an artist, so I can work anywhere. I'd love to open a gallery here in Rosedale. It would be a new, fresh experience in a town that I love." Gabby turns to Judge Joe. "Joe, I want to drive by the house today. I'd like to see what we have to work with."

"Oh, Gabby, that may not be a good idea," John says. "The mansion is in ruins and the cottage needs work."

"I was prepared for that possibility. I guess I'll just have to take it one step at a time. Is the cottage inhabitable?" she asks.

"It is," Sarah responds. "But there's so much that needs to be repaired. Everything is overgrown and I'm sure that nothing has been maintained."

"Then I'll just have to get started right away." Gabby takes a deep breath. "And, Sarah, it's fine that you're curious about Joe and me. The truth is that we both care very much for one another and always have. I've been divorced for quite some time and my children are grown and gone. It's time for me to make a new life and I can't think of a better place than Rosedale. It was my home once, and there's no reason why it can't be again. Bell was my family and stepped up when I needed her most. I can't think of a better way to repay her and maybe lessen her pain."

Suddenly, Jessica and Rob step into the room. Jessica is out of breath. "Sarah! We came as soon as we heard!" She looks at Bell and Emma. "Oh my gosh! That is so sweet! How's she doing?" She lowers her voice.

"She isn't out of danger yet," John answers. "We brought Emma here to see if she might respond." John looks at Gabby. "I'm sorry! Gabby, these are our friends, Jessica and Rob. Jessica and Rob, this is Bell's cousin Gabby who flew in from the East Coast to be with Bell."

"And will be our neighbor," Sarah adds.

"Well, welcome to the neighborhood. How exciting! I'm so sorry that it couldn't be under better circumstances," Jessica says as she reaches out for Gabby's hand and holds it with both of hers.

"Thank you. And thank you for coming here to support us. All we can do is wait," Gabby says as she looks at Bell, still lifeless.

"Gabby wants to take a look at the mansion," Sarah tells Rob. "She's thinking of restoring it." Sarah turns to Gabby. "Gabby, that is a huge job. I'm not sure it's something you'll want to tackle."

Gabby nods her head. "I agree. Perhaps I can start with the cottage. I can stay there with Bell. It's large enough. It's all we really need."

"Gabby, are you talking about the Benton mansion?" Rob asks.

"Why yes. Have you seen it?" Gabby asks.

"I've been looking at homes in the area to restore. I wasn't sure who owned it and took a look at the property. It certainly is a magnificent home. It's a big job, yes, but it would be a grand sight if it was restored properly," Rob says.

"Rob restores homes on the side," John adds. "It's his passion. He's been looking in the area for a project."

"Well, Rob, I'd really appreciate it if you could go out there with us. I'd like your opinion, if you don't mind," Gabby requests.

"I'd love to. You just say the word and we'll take a look around." Rob's face beams.

"If you're available, I'd like to go over there this afternoon. I'm going to have to get a handle on the situation immediately so that I can make some decisions," Gabby says.

"Sarah and John, I would be so grateful if you could join. Rob, we appreciate your valuable input. Does 2:00 p.m. this afternoon work for all of you? That will give Gabby and I time with Bell and we can get Gabby back to the house to rest up," the Judge asks.

"Sure. Jessica? Does that work for you?" Rob turns to Jessica for approval.

"I'd love that. I've never been to the mansion," she answers.

"That works for us, too," John adds.

All of a sudden, Emma barks. "Emma, shhhh!" Gabby turns to settle her down when she sees that Bell is moving. Her eyelids are flickering and she moans. "Look!" Everyone turns to look at Bell who is now moving her fingers. She moans again and then bends her arm and slowly moves it up until she reaches Emma's face. Emma's tail wags wildly and everyone is frozen.

"Bell!" Gabby moves to Bell's bedside. "Bell, it's Gabby. Your cousin Gabby. We're all here for you." Gabby turns to Sarah and John. "She wasn't responding all morning. I can't help but think that Emma made the difference."

Baxter who was laying on the floor sleeping, sits up and barks. "Not you too, Baxter. Shhh!" John orders as he pets the dog's head. "This is a good sign. I'm going to get a nurse." John leaves to get the attention of a nurse outside the room.

Gabby sticks her hand into the oxygen tent and strokes Bell's hand as she continues to touch the fur on Emma's face. Bell opens her eyes slightly and looks at Gabby. She mumbles something and then smiles. Bell then squeezes Gabby's hand and Gabby begins to weep.

Sarah and Jessica begin to tear up. Judge Joe stands behind Gabby and puts his hands on her shoulders, rubbing them affectionately. Gabby turns to look at him. "I think she's going to be alright."

A nurse enters the room. "I brought Doctor Johnson with me."

The doctor enters and pulls the tent slightly open. He looks into Bell's eyes with a light and then listens to her lungs with a stethoscope. "Bell, can you sit up?" Bell moves slightly, indicating that she is making an effort to sit. Gabby and Doctor Johnson help her and the doctor listens to her breathing with the stethoscope on her back.

"Her temperature is going down, and her lungs have improved." The doctor gently lowers Bell back down. "This is a very good sign." He looks at Bell. "Bell, you've got your dog here. You must be one important lady to get your dog into an oxygen tent in ICU!" Everyone laughs and even Bell manages a slight smile.

"I'm hoping that by tomorrow we can get her to eat some soft food. We pumped a lot of fluids in her and it looks like she's rehydrating nicely. That was our biggest battle, along with her temperature. As soon as the antibiotics do their job, we'll get her to sit up and walk a bit to move the fluids in her lungs. But, so far, this is all a very good sign." Bell closes her eyes and smiles. Emma snuggles in next to her.

"Doctor Johnson, we'll take care of Emma. It'd be nice if she can stay a while before we leave. Is that alright?" Sarah asks.

"Yes, I'd say that Emma is doing her job here nicely." Doctor Johnson turns to Judge Joe. "Joe, you and Gabby have been here a long time. Why don't you go home and get some rest? Bell will be fine. You can come back this evening if you'd like. We'll notify you of any changes, but I feel confident that Bell's immune system is starting to take charge. She's going to need a lot of rest. It's going to take time."

"Joe? I think I'm ready for a bit of a rest before we go out to the mansion. Then we can come back here to spend time with Bell," Gabby says.

"Good. I had your things taken to my guest house. You need a good meal and a long rest. John, Sarah, Rob and Jessica, we'll see you at the Benton place at 2:00 p.m." the Judge says as he puts his arm around Gabby who is looking exhausted.

Sarah has a big smile on her face. The Judge gives her a look of satisfaction and joy. "We'll stay here a while so that Emma and Bell can visit." Sarah says. "Emma is going to stay with us until Bell gets well. Gabby, whatever you decide you just let us know. We're happy to keep her for as long as needed."

Bell mumbles and Gabby walks to her bedside and leans over, placing her ear next to her lips. Bell mumbles again and Gabby smiles. "Bell said 'thank the kids.' I think she means 'thank you' for taking Emma."

"Bell, she's in good hands. We'll spoil her with pot pies and everything. You get well so that we can get Emma back to you," Sarah assures her. Bell gives a weak nod and everyone in the room laughs.

"John, Sarah, thank you," Gabby says as she hugs them both.

Judge Joe gives John a strong hand shake and hugs Sarah. Jessica and Rob do the same and everyone except John and Sarah depart.

Alone, Sarah turns to John. "Look." She points to the star.

"Uh huh. So you think that the magical star has something to do with all of this?" John asks.

"Judge Joe himself said it holds great power! I brought it and wished for Bell's recovery and got even more than that! Judge Joe and Gabby are back together!"

"You don't really believe that the star had something to do with it, do you?" John looks at it and gives Sarah a look of skepticism. "You know Judge Joe. He loves to make everything magical."

"And everything is magical. I do believe." Sarah looks at John and grins. "Aren't you the one that told me once that I need to believe? To let go and just have faith?"

"Was that me?" John smiles. "Come here, you!" He grabs Sarah and hugs her. "Yeah, I guess that was me. Thanks for reminding me. Besides, it's Christmas. Anything can happen, right?" John grins and gives her a kiss. "Let's give Emma and Bell some time together and then we'll get back to the house."

John and Sarah sit quietly with Bell who falls back asleep. They can hear her peaceful breathing and Emma, also now sound asleep, begins to snore. The couple look at one another and quietly laugh. They sit, in silence, watching the loving scene until it is time to go.

"John was right," Gabby says as she and Judge Joe pull up to the Benton mansion. "It's a disaster. It's shocking, actually." They sit in silence for a few minutes, looking at the decayed home until Rob and

Jessica pull up behind them. John and Sarah can be seen opening the front door and stepping onto the large porch.

Rob walks to Gabby's passenger window which she puts down. "You ready? I hope that you're wearing comfortable, flat boots. The ground is unstable and I'm afraid the flooring in the house is too. We'll have to be careful."

"Yes, I'm prepared," Gabby answers. Judge Joe and Gabby exit their car and join the couple as they walk up the overgrown walkway paving a path through the snow that has built up. "I haven't seen this place since I was young," Gabby says as she navigates brush and weeds. "It's so sad to see it like this. It was such a grand, elegant home."

"I haven't been out here in many years myself," Judge Joe says as he steps on the brush. He puts his arm around Gabby's waist, assisting her along the uneven walkway. They look at one another with a sad, but reassuring smile. The four reach the porch and join John and Sarah.

"Welcome, Gabby. John and I took a quick tour of the place yesterday. It was open and we had to make sure that Bell wasn't here. That's when we found her at the back property." Sarah looks at Gabby who is taking it all in. "Gabby, would you like to do the honors? I'm sure you know the place better than anyone."

Gabby looks up at the tall columns and the peeling exterior. She takes a deep breath, steps forward, and turns the knob of the front door. It grudgingly opens. She takes a step inside as the rest of the group watches.

"It's O.K. Please. Come in," Gabby motions them to follow her.

The group carefully enters. The home is eerily silent. The three couples stand in the foyer looking at the dingy and decayed interior. The high ceilings boast ornate crown molding and the walls still hold expensive and detailed portraits coated with a thick layer of dust.

"Gabby? It's your show," Judge Joe says, "What would you like to see first?"

Gabby looks around the entrance and is drawn to the left side where there are two large, pocket doors. She walks over and slides them open. Inside the dark room is beautiful antique furniture with velvet material and ornate legs. The heavy draperies are faded and packed with dirt. Gabby pulls them open. A big waft of dust explodes into the air, causing her to cough.

"This is where wonderful parties were held," she says. Overhead is a large chandelier, now dull and so heavily coated with dust that it looks like grey fur. "Bell's debutante party was held here. I was just a child and I watched from those doors. She points to a second set of pocket doors on the opposite side of the room. "I slid them open just so slightly and peeked through. The women were so beautifully dressed with their white gloves. Music played and there was so much joy. It was a magical time." She looks around the room as though reliving the scene. The others watch as she recalls the memories.

Gabby turns to Judge Joe. "I hear that Bell Cottage is completely hidden and overgrown."

"Bell Cottage?" Sarah asks.

"Yes. That's the home that Prescott built for them. He named it 'Bell Cottage' for obvious reasons."

"The bell," Sarah says to John. He nods.

"That makes sense since it looks like she hasn't so much as set foot in this house for years," Rob comments.

John and Sarah nod "The cottage has been neglected, but Bell has kept the interior clean and actually quite nice," John shares.

"Rob, it looks like the main house is going to take a major overhaul. Is that something that you would be interested in getting involved with? Since you're the expert in restoring older homes, I'd love your thoughts. Is it past saving?"

"Gabby, this home is such a treasure and it deserves to shine just like it once did. It's my passion and working on the Benton mansion would be a dream come true." Rob is noticeably excited.

"Then I'll leave it to you to explore the home and come back to me with your ideas and, of course, what you think it would cost to get this place back in order. My guess is that this is a long-term project."

"You're looking at easily two years to get it back to working condition," Rob says. "That's just getting all of the basics in order like the electrical, plumbing, and structure. Then there's the woodworking and, well, I don't want to overwhelm you. I think you get the picture."

"I figured as much. I'll let you get to assessing the damages. Now let's go check on the cottage." Gabby walks back into the hallway, past the staircase and to the back of the house. She steps into the kitchen. "Like going back in time. It's as though she just left one day and never came back." She walks to the pantry and looks through cupboards. "When her parents got older, she took care of them in this house. When they died, my guess is that she walked back to the cottage and never stepped foot in here again. Just left everything."

Jessica and Rob walk around the kitchen, exploring. "I think that it could be beautiful again. It certainly seems to be well built," Jessica comments.

"Oh it was. It was appointed the best of everything. My Aunt and Uncle hired servants and cooks and groundskeepers. They spoiled all of us." Gabby turns the faucet which sputters and spits, giving up a single drop. "Rob, this is a big challenge! I don't know how you're going to manage it."

"Don't you worry, Gabby. I'll take care of everything." Rob looks at Jessica and smiles.

Gabby heads out the back door and into the backyard that stretches for well over an acre to the wooded area at the end of the property. Like Sarah and John, they make their way through the brush, following the path that John cut until they reach the cottage.

"It's adorable!" Jessica walks to the front of the home and examines it. "Under all of that ivy is beautiful stonework!"

"It *is* lovely," Gabby agrees. "It was made with love." She looks at the Judge who takes her hand and squeezes it. They look at each other and smile. "We can get this in top shape for Bell before she comes home. Joe, can we get a crew out here to work on this?"

"My dear, we can get you anything you please. I know some great contractors and I can have them over here today. You let me take care of everything." Judge Joe pats her hand affectionately.

Gabby steps onto the stone stoop and enters the home. Just as before, they see the well maintained furniture and wall hangings. The couples walk around the home, checking each room. The kitchen is clean and neat as is the rest of the home. Everything is perfectly in place.

"She obviously loves this home," Gabby comments. "Joe, I've seen enough. Let's get your contractors over here to spruce up the exterior and fix anything inside that may need updates."

"Your wish is my command." The Judge looks at Rob and Jessica. "Thank you so much for coming out here with us. Rob, feel free to look around the property and let us know your thoughts. I think the Benton mansion is worth saving." He pauses and turns to John and Sarah. "And to you, what can I say? Words can not express. . . "tears well up in his eyes.

"And you don't have to. We only did what we were guided to do." Sarah takes the Judge's hand. "No coincidences, right?"

He smiles. "No coincidences."

"Let's get out of here," Gabby says. "I want to get back to the hospital and then, Joe, how about if I cook you a nice dinner this evening?"

"Gabby, I'd take you up on that, but not tonight. You've been through a lot these past 24 hours and you deserve to relax. I have a chef who will cook us anything we want!" The Judge looks at

Sarah and winks. He puts his arm around Gabby and guides her out of the home and down the porch steps. Gabby gives him an affectionate smile. Her body relaxes as he holds her.

Jessica and Rob head back to the house where they happily explore each room. The Judge and Gabby return to Bell's bedside and John and Sarah make their way home.

Chapter Twelve
An Even Bigger Surprise

"Little Emma is such a good girl," Sarah says as she walks out of her office. The portly Terrier closely follows her.

"She's one *spoiled* pup!" John shouts from his office.

Sarah walks to the entrance of John's office with a stack of papers. "Well, tomorrow's Christmas Eve. Did we decide what to do for our anniversary?"

John gives her a clever grin. "Are you O.K. with surprises?"

"My life is one big surprise after another lately. Why? Do you have something in mind?" Sarah sits down in the chair across from John.

"Perhaps. If you're willing to put me in charge, I'd like to plan the evening." Baxter lays at John's feet, sleeping.

"Sure. Why not?" Emma jumps in Sarah's lap. "I spoke with Gabby this morning and she told me that Bell is recovering quite well. It looks like she'll be released tomorrow and home for Christmas!"

"That's great. I know that Gabby and the Judge have been getting her place fixed up. She's going to be so surprised and so pleased," John says.

"Yeah, and Rob's been working with Gabby to get started on the Benton mansion. He's pretty excited about it." Sarah pets Emma.

"It couldn't have worked out better. He's had his eye on that place for some time." John leans forward and places his elbows on the desk. "Speaking of Rob and the mansion, I was thinking of going over there to help out. He has some contractors there and could use my assistance. It'd be nice to spend some guy time with him," John raises his eyebrows waiting for Sarah's response.

"Like you even have to ask! Of course. I'll wrap things up here and you can head out. I have plenty of things to take care of," Sarah places Emma on the floor and stands.

John walks to her and gives her a kiss. "Thanks, hon. I'll see you later on, back at the house. I'll take Baxter with me."

"Samantha!" Sarah shouts. "Can you please come in here?"

Samantha appears at the doorway. "You need more coffee Sarah?"

Sarah smiles. "No, Samantha. John and I want to give you your Christmas gift. We're closing up the office early and since tomorrow is Christmas Eve, we'd like to send you home."

"Oh, that is a very nice Christmas gift, Miss Sarah!" Samantha smiles.

"That's not the gift," John laughs. He pulls open the top drawer of his desk. "This is the gift." John hands her an envelope.

"Oh wait! I have your Christmas card in the other room too!" Samantha starts to walk out the door.

"Samantha, just stay right here and open your envelope," John orders.

Samantha is reluctant, looking embarrassed, and slowly opens it up. She looks at the front of the card, a sparkling pine tree in snow. "Oh that is a very nice card! Very pretty with the sparkles! Thank you!"

"Samantha, look inside," John says as he and Sarah snicker.

"There's more?" Samantha opens the envelope and pulls out a piece of paper that is tucked inside it. She opens the paper and reads it. "Oh Miss Sarah, Mr. John! This is too much! Too much!"

"It's not too much, Samantha. You've been a wonderful Assistant and John and I are grateful for all of the work you've done in our first year of business. We want you and your husband to go away for a long weekend, at a retreat in the mountains. Spend time together. There's a certificate for the entire weekend including dinner and the spa. All you have to do is get there. You've earned it and so does your husband whose put up with all of the evenings you've spent here, helping us on cases."

Samantha steps to Sarah and gives her a hug. "Oh Miss Sarah, Mr. John, I *love* working here. You are so generous! Thank you!" She walks to John and hugs him.

"Now go! Get out of here and spend time with your family. We'll see you after Christmas!" John orders.

Samantha is beaming. "Thank you!" She walks back into the reception area, still looking at the certificate for a weekend in the mountains. "Oh! So nice! So nice!" She packs up her things and heads to the door. "Merry Christmas Miss Sarah, Mr. John! Merry Christmas!

"Well," John turns to Sarah, "I'm going to pack up. It looks like our Christmas has begun."

John and Sarah gather their belongings, Baxter, Emma, and head out of the office.

"I'm so excited!" Sarah shouts as she descends down the staircase. She is wearing a little black dress and faux fur wrap, high heels and a sparkly broach in her hair that is pulled up in an elegant French twist.

"You should be!" John says as he stands at the dining room table placing a bottle of champagne in a carry bag. He is wearing a tuxedo and looking as handsome as ever.

"You look as incredible as you did on our wedding day!" Sarah exclaims.

"Thank you, my dear. This is, in fact, the same tuxedo!" He grins. "You look stunning. Get over here!" He grabs her hand and pulls her close. She laughs. "Happy anniversary, Mrs. Rivera." He gives her a long kiss.

"Happy anniversary darling. A whole year!" They hold each other and Sarah moves away. "O.K., so what is this big surprise?"

"Oh, you'll find out soon enough, but this will require a blind fold." He says as he picks up a scarf laying on the table.

"Are you kidding?" She looks at it with wide eyes.

"No, I'm not. I'll put it on you when we get in the car. Now you have to promise me that you won't peek, and you'll go along with this." John walks to the closet and pulls out their overcoats. "It's critical to the surprise and I don't want you to ruin it."

"O.K. I promise, but I can't imagine what you're up to!" Sarah says as John slides her coat on her.

John puts on his coat and grabs the champagne. He walks Sarah to the car and places the blindfold on her.

"This is totally crazy," Sarah laughs. "There aren't any places that I can think of that would be a surprise in Rosedale!"

"Oh, we'll see about that," John states with confidence. They drive for a few minutes and Sarah is still unable to guess the destination.

"Is it Mr. Landis's house? That is, after all, where we were married!" Sarah states.

"Like I'm going to tell you!" John teases. "You don't have any clue, do you?"

"No! This is driving me nuts! What on earth?" Sarah laughs and enjoys the mystery.

Soon, John stops the car and there is silence. "Stay right there. I'm coming over to get you out." He walks over to Sarah's door and helps her out of the car, keeping her blindfold on. He holds her around the waist and they slowly walk on what appears to be a sidewalk. "Keep walking. We're almost there." They stop. "Now I'm going to help you up three steps," he announces. They navigate up stairs and Sarah can hear John open a door. She steps onto a floor in . . . a restaurant? A house? It's difficult to tell, but still it is completely silent. "We're going to walk over a few more steps and then we can take off the blindfold."

John walks Sarah into place. "One, two, three," and he pulls off the blindfold.

"SURPRISE! HAPPY ANNIVERSARY!" Sarah opens her eyes to see an entire room full of people, all dressed in black tie attire and holding champagne glasses! Above her is a large, sparkling chandelier and the floor is covered in a fine Turkish carpet. It is the Benton mansion drawing room. The same room where Bell had her debutante party. Before her, in the front of the guests who crowd around, sits Bell with Emma on her lap. Bell is holding a glass of champagne in the air with a big smile on her face.

"Bell!" Sarah walks to the elderly woman who looks ten years younger. She wears a feminine, red dress, pearls and her hair is cut and curled. Her cheeks are rosy and her face beams with joy. "You look lovely! I'm so glad to see you!" Bell smiles and squeezes Sarah's hand.

Jessica walks up to Sarah along with Rob, and Mr. and Mrs. Wright. "Happy anniversary, my friend! This wasn't an easy one to keep a secret!" Jessica says.

Rob laughs. "No it wasn't! I'm proud of her!"

"So, that time that John was spending over here, you were getting this all fixed up?" Sarah stands in amazement as she looks around the perfect room now sparkling and clean as though brand new.

"Yeah. Come with me." John grabs her hand and walks her back to the front porch. It is completely renovated, no longer rotted and sagging. The columns are painted and strong, wrapped with roping and lights. A small Christmas tree is on the porch, fully decorated and lit.

"This is beautiful!" Sarah exclaims. Gabby and Judge Joe join them. "Gabby, you must be so proud!"

"Happy anniversary you two! And, yes, I am *very* proud and pleased. Rob did most of the work along with a crew of contractors. The house has a long way to go, but we focused on the drawing room. John told me about your dream and I think it has some significance. It was John's idea to have the surprise anniversary here." Gabby shares.

"But, Sarah, we have an even bigger surprise!" Judge Joe says. He turns to Gabby and lifts her left hand. On it is a large, diamond ring.

"Get out! You're engaged!" Sarah shouts and runs to Gabby, giving her a big hug.

Judge Joe belts out a big laugh. "Oh that's just part of it." He looks over at John who walks back into the foyer and reappears with a bouquet of flowers handing it to Gabby.

"Sarah, would you do me the honor of being my bridesmaid tonight?" Gabby says as she holds the bouquet in front of her and extends it to Sarah.

"What?" Sarah blinks and stares, trying to comprehend the request.

"Right now, here in this house, in that room, Gabby and I will be wed and if you agree, we'd like you and John to stand up with us. Bell has agreed to be Maid of Honor, and your Dad, Sarah, is my Best Man,'" Judge Joe announces.

Sarah looks at Gabby who has a big smile on her face. "Sometimes it's just right," Gabby smiles. "We've waited a long time for this and we couldn't think of a better night than Christmas Eve."

Sarah begins to cry. "I can't believe you pulled this off! This is the most incredible gift for all of us! Yes! Yes, of course! You have my blessing!" Sarah accepts the bouquet.

"Excellent!" Gabby hugs Sarah. "Now before the hoopla starts, there is one more thing that I need to do." Gabby walks into the foyer and everyone follows. On a table in the entrance is a gift, wrapped in red foil paper and a big, white bow. "Rob, this is for you." Rob has a total look of surprise and steps over to accept the gift. "Please, open it now. I want everyone to see it."

Speechless, Rob accepts the gift and unwraps it. Inside is a wooden plaque with a gold, metal inset. He removes it from the box and examines it. On the gold plaque are two words, "Villa Bellissima."

"In Italy, each home is given a name and I did the honors of naming the Benton mansion. John and Sarah, you gave me the best gift. You gave me my Bell for Christmas. Rob, you worked so hard to restore this house to make this day so special." She turns and looks around. Even the stair case has been restored. "I can't think of a better person to own it than you."

"What?!" Sarah's mouth drops open.

"Yes, Bell and I have no use for this big place, and I saw how much Rob loved it so he has agreed to purchase it. Bell will continue to own and live in Bell Cottage. We're splitting up the property. I know that in a few years, it will again be the grandest home in all of Rosedale. Villa Bellissima will no longer be a house, it will become a home."

"This is the best gift. I can't think of a better name than "Villa Bellissima." Rob's eyes tear up and Jessica walks to his side, putting her arm around his waist.

The group turns to see a small figure join them. Bell approaches, guided by Mr. Landis and followed by Emma. Bell extends her hand to Rob and he holds it and kisses her cheek.

"She's thankful too, Rob," Gabby shares.

Bell then walks over to Sarah and puts her arms out for a hug. Sarah gently embraces her and John joins them.

"We've arranged for Bell to live in the cottage. We have a nurse checking on her, and I'll be spending a lot of time there, of course. Sarah and John, Bell wanted me to tell you how thankful she is," Gabby shares.

John leans down and picks up Emma. "And it started out with a little dog rescue!" They all laugh. "I guess we don't have to worry about that now!"

"Well? Is everyone ready? Let's get this wedding started!" Judge Joe bellows out. The group cheers. "John, you're on deck!"

"Ready!" John responds. He hands Bell a bouquet of flowers that rest on the foyer table and waves at the Minister who stands at the front of the room. He waves back and nods to a stringed quartet that sits in the corner of the room, which begins to play.

"Ladies and gentlemen, may we convene? Gather around and leave an aisle for the bride to enter," the Minister loudly announces. The room is filled with neighbors and friends who excitedly chat and part to form a center aisle. John turns and walks back to Bell.

As the crowd settles down, John and Mr. Wright escort Bell slowly down the aisle to the front of the room where the Minister stands. The men hold Bell steady as Judge Joe joins them. Sarah appears, walking slowly with a huge smile on her face, the bouquet of flowers in her hand. She stands opposite John and Judge Joe who are beaming with joy.

Gabby then enters, looking radiant in a white, long flowing dress, holding a bouquet of red and white flowers. She is laughing and smiling as she joins the wedding party and Judge Joe. The entire room can see that the two are deeply in love. Judge Joe takes Gabby's hand in his and the Minister begins the ceremony.

"Ladies and Gentlemen! Thank you for joining in this joyous celebration. All of you who know the story of Joe and Gabby, must be in awe at the the power of love. This ceremony is a reminder that true love never dies and that faith and patience prevail. Not only has Gabby regained her family," the Minister smiles and looks at Bell, "but, a new family has been created. I am sure that you all join in blessing these two and supporting them in their new life together, here in Rosedale." The Minister looks at Gabby. "Gabby, welcome back. And and welcome, Bell and Gabby, to your new family, the town of Rosedale." The Minister motions to the audience that breaks out in applause. Everyone stands and continues to clap and cheer.

Judge Joe smiles and nods to the Minister who continues, shouting over the applause. "Joe Conner! Gabriella Benton! Do you take one another in good times and bad, sickness and health. . ." Judge Joe cuts him off.

"We do!" the Judge shouts.

Gabby laughs loudly. "We do!" She puts her arms around Judge Joe and they kiss.

A BELL FOR CHRISTMAS

"Well, I guess that's it! I now pronounce you husband and wife!" The Minister laughs and places his hands on their shoulders then raises them to the sky and shakes his head.

Bell smiles and clasps her hands. Mr. Wright leans down and takes the rings off of Emma's collar and hands them to the couple. Still laughing, they take the rings and place them on one another. Judge Joe takes Gabby and turns her toward the audience, lifting her hand in the air with his. The audience, once again, cheers loudly and claps.

Sarah, John, and Mr. Wright are all laughing and Bell smiles. The wedded couple make their way back down the aisle and the wedding party, still at the front of the room, hug one another.

"Come on!" John says. He and Mr. Wright slowly walk Bell back to the entrance of the room where the bride and groom stand, greeting everyone.

Bell turns to Sarah and points. "Bell, what? John, stop. Bell wants to say something." The men stop and Sarah leans close. Bell mumbles and points to the string quartet in the corner, then points to herself. "Bell, would you like to sit by the quartet for a while?" Bell nods her head. "Dad, John, let's take Bell over there so that she can enjoy the music." Mr. Wright and John walk her to the corner of the room and place a chair close to the musicians. Bell nods her head and smiles. They seat her and make their way toward the foyer, where Judge Joe and Gabby stand, hugging and chatting with the guests.

"Well? Was this a good anniversary celebration?" John asks. He stops, taking both of Sarah's hands in his. "Were you surprised?"

"It couldn't have been a better day. I'm still in shock. John, when did you know? I mean, about Judge Joe and Gabby?" Sarah asks.

"Well, after Joe and Gabby checked out the mansion and cottage, they had dinner at his place. As Judge Joe told me, he knew he had to ask for Gabby's hand. He didn't want to wait. As you can see, she accepted. It couldn't have been better timing. They got started fixing up Bell's place, and the main house. Gabby wanted to get married here, so Rob got busy. I helped out, getting it ready for the ceremony. We really hustled! I wanted to surprise you and Judge Joe and Gabby loved the idea!"

"Well, I love the idea, too. My gosh, it looks fabulous!" Sarah looks around. "More than anything, I'm surprised that Judge Joe is now a married man! And the mansion! Rob will get to restore this incredible place, Bell gets her cottage, this is a dream! All from a little dog!" They both look across the room at little Emma, still seated next to Bell.

"Oh John! I wish I had Bell's gift!" Sarah turns to him.

"Not to worry. I was prepared. Come on." John walks Sarah to the foyer where, on the entrance table is a beautifully wrapped gift in white paper and a gold ribbon. "Here. I knew we'd need this tonight."

"Thank you!" Sarah kisses him and takes the gift in her hand. She looks toward Bell who, looking peaceful, listens to the quartet, her eyes closed and a smile on her face. A gentleman stands in back of Bell's chair smiling. Sarah, clears her eyes and looks again. "Prescott?"

"What?" John looks at Sarah who is staring at Bell.

"John, look. There, standing next to Bell!" Sarah points.

"Next to Bell? No one's standing next to Bell." John stares at the corner and sees Bell, Emma, and the musician's playing.

Prescott smiles at Sarah and nods his head. She nods back, turns and grabs John's hand. "Come with me. We need to go over there!" Sarah pushes through the dense crowd of people. She loses sight of Bell, but pushes through until she finally arrives. There sits Bell and Emma on their own.

"Oh!" Sarah looks around. "Bell, I was just looking for the man that was standing here with you." She continues to scan the room. Bell looks at her and smiles, saying nothing. "I swore," Sarah looks at John, confused.

John watches her for a moment, realizing that she is serious. "Bell, sorry. Sarah thought she saw someone she knew." He apologizes.

Sarah stands for a moment, staring at the space around Bell who continues to look at her with a peaceful smile. "Sorry," she says and pauses. "For a moment, I thought," Sarah stops and shakes her head as though clearing out her thoughts. She regains her composure and turns back to Bell. "Bell, John and I have a gift for you. It's actually something we're returning to you. Well, you'll see what I mean. Please open it."

Sarah hands Bell the beautiful package which she places on her lap. Bell looks at it for a moment and begins to slowly unwrap it. She removes the top and tissue paper, stares and blinks. Tears stream down her face. She picks up the object and holds it up. In her hand is the bell that Sarah found at the cottage, no longer tarnished. It shines brightly, clearly displaying the etched words "Bell Cottage, With Love Eternal, Prescott."

"Bell, I hope you like it. I found it buried in the snow and I thought it should be restored and put in its proper place, the entrance of Bell Cottage. I hope you're pleased." Sarah waits for her response.

Bell stares at the item with a look of love and sadness. She extends her hand toward Sarah who takes Bell's hand in hers. Their eyes connect and Bell nods with a smile.

"Bell, we'll leave you to enjoy the music," Sarah says. Bell squeezes Sarah's hand and nods, with a look of joy that Sarah had not seen before. John and Sarah leave her and walk back to the wedded couple. Sarah looks back to see Bell looking behind her and cupping her hand against her mouth as though telling a secret to someone. Sarah continues to watch Bell and sees Prescott, once again, standing behind her. He is leaning down, listening to Bell and then stands. He looks at Sarah and nods his head at her with a big smile on his face.

Sarah smiles and laughs to herself. Bell and Prescott both wave at her.

"What? What are you laughing at?" John asks as they walk into the foyer to join the guests.

"Oh nothing," Sarah smiles and waves back at the couple. "Nothing at all." John turns and looks back to see what Sarah is watching and shrugs his shoulders.

Mr. and Mrs. Wright greet Sarah and John, congratulating them. "Another exciting Christmas Eve!" Mrs. Wright says.

"It's going to be tough to top this one," Mr. Wright adds.

Gabby walks up to Sarah. "I have something of yours, Sarah." She has a small satchel with a drawstring that she hands over.

"A gift? That's not necessary," Sarah says.

"Not exactly. Open it," Gabby gestures to the satchel with a smile.

Sarah opens it and looks inside. She reaches in and pulls out the Christmas star.

"I hear that you're the rightful owner." Gabby places her hands on Sarah's. "I have the feeling that there'll be many good uses for it in the future. You take care of the star, and I'll take care of my Bell." Gabby, grins. Sarah smiles before giving her a big hug.

"Gabby, I'm so pleased for your new beginning with Bell, Rosedale and most of all, Judge Joe!" Sarah says.

"A toast is in order!" Judge Joe shouts over the noisy room. "Everyone!" he bellows out, raising his champagne glass. "To new beginnings!"

"To new beginnings!" Everyone shouts, clinking glasses around the room.

"To new beginnings," Gabby says. She clinks his glass and smiles.

Conclusion

"Careful up there!" John shouts, looking at Rob who is high up on a ladder at Villa Bellissima.

"Oh, I'm secured. It looks scary, but I'm locked in here!" Rob shouts back. "What are you two doing here? Coming to visit?"

"Coming to drop off some muffins for Bell, and a couple of pot pies!" Sarah shouts back.

"Did you put in your notice?" John yells.

"Yes! You know the law firm wasn't very happy to lose another attorney so soon! It seems to be a habit in this town!"

Sarah laughs. "Well, we're sorry about that, but John and I are pleased to launch Rivera, Rivera and Frost in the new year. Are you ready for all of this?"

"Yeah! Between law and the restoration, it's going to be a busy new year!"

Suddenly, Jessica sticks her head out of the upper story window. "What are y'all shouting about out here!"

"Hey Jessica!" Sarah yells.

"Did you see the plaque?" Jessica points to the front porch.

To the right of the front door is the gold plaque Gabby gifted Rob. "Villa Bellissima" is etched on it. "It's perfect!" Sarah waves. "We're on our way back to visit Bell and Emma. Want to join?"

"Yeah! I'd love to. Rob? Take a break!" Jessica orders. Rob climbs down his ladder and Jessica comes out the front door. Behind them a furry pup bounces out. The dog runs up to Sarah and John and jumps.

"Who is this?" Sarah bends down and gives the dog a big hug.

"That's Rufus! We wanted to honor the Rosedale Rescue. They are, after all, how all of this got started.

"Welcome to the family, Rufus!" John pets the dog who jumps up and down. John looks at Sarah. "This is a Christmas none of us will ever forget."

"No, we won't. Happy anniversary, honey. And many more," Sarah smiles and grabs John's hand.

"And many more." John leans over and kisses her. "Well? Shall we? There's a special lady and her dog waiting for their pot pies. The four walk to the back of the property, now cleared and pristine. In plain sight is the fairy tale, stone cottage restored and looking new.

The friends put their arms around each others shoulders as they walk toward the cottage. As they near, the front door opens and little Emma runs out. Bell waves and they gather on the front stoop, chatting as she welcomes them in. They enter the cottage and the front door closes. The shiny bell hanging next to the front door excitedly rings.

THE END . . . for Now

CPSIA information can be obtained
at www.ICGtesting.com
Printed in the USA
LVHW110032200919
631651LV00014B/11/P

9 781478 776369